TALES OF A NUMINOUS NATURE
A Short Story Collection

By
Violette L. Meier

VIORI PUBLISHING

VIORI PUBLISHING
P.O. Box 5283
Atlanta, GA 31107

ISBN: 978-0-9887805-8-3

Printed in the United States of America

Cover Photography by Xoe Reid
Cover Designed by Viori Publishing

DEDICATED

...to God. You are therefore I am.

...to my great grandmother Ma Sadie. It was because of you that my imagination began to flower.

...to my mother and Aunt Ruth who are the epitome of beauty.

...to my loving husband, all our children, and our family. You are the reason why I do what I do. I love you!

AUTHOR'S NOTE

This book is special to me because most of these stories were written when I was between the ages of 15-25. I was learning myself. I present this book to you as unaltered as I possibly can so you can grasp my vision during that time of my life. Enjoy...if you dare!

TALES OF A NUMINOUS NATURE

A Short Story Collection

TABLE OF CONTENTS

AFRAID OF THE DARK

Cindee Layne sat up in her bed; her body flinging up so fast that it seemed as if an invisible force was tossing her into the air. Her light was off! Fear and anger flooded her being for everyone in her house knew that the dark was her nemesis and that she kept the lamp on in the far corner of her room to guard against her overactive imagination.

Cindee was a vivid dreamer and if she opened her eyes to a black room, the evils of her cerebral would dance before her eyes as crisp and clear as television actors. Usually it was the same cloaked creature, sitting upon her dresser with its beady eyes burning and its crooked hands fondling its bent legs, waiting to ravish her with its perverse wickedness.

Luckily tonight was a dreamless one, but the darkness woke her anyway, beckoning her out of her peaceful sleep like a potential lover nudging his sweetheart softly as she slumbered.

Light panic shortened her breath as her yellow brown eyes tried to make sense out of the shadows. With determination and a deep inhale and a shallow exhale, she bolted to the corner and clicked the lamp switch. Nothing.

Heavy creases adorned her forehead. One by one the hairs on the back of her neck erected themselves like dominoes in reverse. She quickly unscrewed the light bulb and shook the small white glass close to her ear. A tiny tingling noise rattled inside of the thin glass. The bulb was blown. Cindee placed the bulb in her pajama pocket and bolted for the door as if an entity was after her. At any moment she expected to feel its hands upon her shoulders.

She reached the dark hallway and flicked on the light. Her fear subsided just a bit as she rambled through the hall closet searching for a new bulb. She found nothing. Disappointed, she turned the corner and headed straight to her brother's room.

Quietly, Cindee pushed open the door; her hands like bright gold against the mahogany wood. The hall light spilled into the room casting the messy chamber her slumbering brother inhabited in a pale glow.

She crept silently against the wall, careful not to wake her elder brother by tumbling over one of many objects he failed to pick up in his waking life. She appeared before one of the many small lamps sitting on a long table connected to the wall.

Her tiny fingers slipped through one of the cone shaped shades and wrapped around a bulb. Her fingers caressed the thin glass as she steadied her frantic breaths. She twisted it quickly and dislodged it and switched his good bulb with her blown one. After making the swap, she walked slowly back to her room, preparing herself to enter the darkness. Her breathing became more and more labored as she drew closer to her bedroom door. Shadows played in the corners of her eyes. More than once she jumped because she swore some otherworldly thing was lingering near.

Cindee needed to remain calm. Her sanity depended on it. After all, she was seventeen, nearly a grown woman and she knew her room like the back of her hand yet her fear of the darkness was crushing down on her like the foot of a giant. The uncanny feeling that she was not alone in the darkness made her crazy. So real was the presence that dwelled in the realm between her imagination and her room, Cindee felt as if she could reach out and touch it. She imagined its beady eyes resting upon her as she neared her door; its sinewy body perched up on her dresser like a bird ready to swoop down and attack her with jagged talons.

Her fear elevated. Couldn't she just sleep in the hallway? The thought did not seem like a bad one but she put it away from her mind. She was being childish. No way was she going to give her siblings more ammunition to play cruel jokes on her. She could imagine them stealing her bulbs on a nightly basis or turning the lamp off and jumping out of her closet when she got out of bed to turn it back on. No! She would not give them the satisfaction.

Cindee ran into her bedroom so fast that she nearly pulled her little toe off when she banged it on the edge of her vanity. A tear rolled down the corner of her eye but she refused to fall to the floor, limping wholeheartedly towards the small lamp. Her aching foot dragged against the carpet feeling like a match getting ready to ignite.

Her skin felt like a cloak. She could feel it all over her. Chill bumps raced down her arms in currents of chilled flesh and prickly hairs. The darkness felt like a tangible blanket being wrapped around her tighter and tighter with every step that she took. More tears began to swell in her large oval eyes. Her long lashes blurred her vision as they caught tiny droplets of water. The faster she walked, the further the little lamp seemed and the closer she seemed to be coming to the thing that cloaked itself in the blackness of her room.

She froze. She thought she heard movement. A low whine escaped her lips. She sprinted now. Cindee could not afford to let her imagination get the best of her.

When her heart was on the brink of explosion and her mind teetering on insanity, the little lamp sat right before her trembling fingers. Cindee grabbed the little brass desk light with her right hand and retrieved the bulb out of her pocket with her left hand. Her fingers clung to the glass bulb so tight that she was afraid that it would shatter and bloody her clammy fingers. With a shaky exhale, she forced the bulb into the lamp and twisted it in with hard, wrist paining turns. She flipped the switch. The room blazed with soft yellow light. The fear crawled back into the recesses of her mind followed by the creature biding its sweet time.

ARROGANCE

"Evil. No one knows what evil truly is until staring at the author of deception face to face. I met evil one night dressed in the garments of a poor man. His demeanor was at first humble and sincere until he showed me his face. His true face," the man screamed at the calm psychiatrist sitting in front of him, his spittle flying everywhere. "I'm not crazy!"

The doctor sat quietly, unblinking, listening to the mad man in the straitjacket sitting in front of her rave. She wiped the slobber from her note pad with a tissue and tossed the soiled paper in the trash. The doctor ran her fingers through her curly dark hair and leaned back against her chair, trying to relax herself. Her white coat was luminescent against her dark skin. She placed her pointer finger against her chin and took a deep breath.

"Tell me your story Mr. Dole." She leaned forward in her chair. "Be calm. I don't think that you are crazy," she replied.

Mr. Dole un-stretched his red rimmed eyes and began to rock slowly back and forth while humming quietly under his breath.

"Do you really believe me?" he asked as his water filled eyes stared into the eyes of the doctor. "Really?"

"Yes," she answered. She paused. "Tell me your story."

The man leaned back against the gray cushioned chair and sighed. He shook his sweaty hair and stretched his neck.

"Ahhh," he purred after the stretch.

"Would you like some water?" the doctor asked.

"Yes ma'am."

A man wearing all white placed a paper cup to Mr. Dole's mouth and allowed him to take a sip.

"Thank you," Mr. Dole replied, a look of uneasiness on his face. The man in white's eyes was almost crystal clear. It looked as if his pupils were a dot on ice cubes.

The doctor nodded and the man in white resumed his position standing behind the doctor's chair; his cold eyes sill affixed on Mr. Dole.

Mr. Dole shook off a chill and forced his eyes on the doctor.

"Mr. Dole," the doctor said. "Tell me of evil."

Mr. Dole leaned back in his seat and tried his best to relax but between the discomfort of his straitjacket and the eyes of the medical assistant, relaxing was difficult. He took a deep breath and began to speak.

"A few weeks ago, I was at home in the kitchen with my wife. I can remember that she wore a red nightgown. You know the sexy kind." He smiled. "I bought it for her the night before. That night was spectacular." He raised his eyebrows and winked at the doctor. The doctor smiled. Mr. Dole continued. "Anyhow, she stood over the stove fixing us breakfast and I got up from the table and kissed her neck. After a wonderful meal, we both got dressed and headed to work; me to my office and her to her errands." Mr. Dole paused and helplessly licked at a tear that his hands were prevented from wiping.

"Go ahead Mr. Dole," the doctor said as she crossed her curvy legs and adjusted her jacket.

"I worked hard that day at the office. I was so frustrated and fed up that I took an early lunch and had a few drinks with the fellas. Of course the entire time I was boasting about my latest accomplishments and how I was simply the best at everything. My co-workers agreed completely. While we were at the bar praising my achievements, this strange man came up to me and smiled. I can remember his devious eyes and toothless grin just like it was yesterday. He smelled of dead flesh, sewage back-up, rotten eggs, and every other unbearable odor you could imagine. He then sat next to me. The other two men with me were just as astonished as I was to witness the audacity of this person." Mr. Dole's voice got louder. He leaned forward in his chair and stared into the doctor's eyes. "Could you imagine the balls?" he asked and leaned back.

The doctor smiled. "Please continue," she asked as she inserted her ink pen into her mouth; nibbling the pen top.

Mr. Dole tossed his stringy hair back. "You know that I wouldn't kill a fly. Why am I wearing this jacket?" he asked realizing that he would not receive a response. He smacked his invisible lips and continued his story.

"This man sat next to me and smiled. I put my glass down and asked him what he wanted. He looked at me and said, 'I came to challenge you.' Challenge me in what I asked him. Surely he could not compare in intelligence or physical strength. I was very physically fit and intellectually competent. He was a sloppy looking moron who didn't have wits enough to get a job and get off the streets or to wash his funky hide. My friends and I laughed. I finally restrained myself from dying of hysteria and asked the man his game. The toothless gent simply smiled and said, 'I have power, true power. I have strength to conquer all,' he said as his rank breath offended my nose. Well you should have enough power to wash yourself. I told him as my friends and I laughed and ridiculed him.

"The man's eyes narrowed. He stood up and pointed his filthy finger in my face. 'I challenge you!' he bellowed as I sat there becoming more annoyed by the second by this obviously insane individual. My pride would not let me dismiss this man. I always needed validation for being the best at everything and I was not mentally equipped to pass up a challenge no matter how ludicrous. I looked at my friends and back to the contentious cretin in front of me, reeking of putrid funk. I smiled a facetious smile and asked the halfwit his game. The imbecile said that he could outdo me in anything. I looked over to my friends again. They lifted and dropped their shoulders, saying nothing. I stood up, removed my gray tweed jacket, and adjusted my navy blue tie. I ran my fingers through my hair and shook my shoulders. I finally finished my cocky presentation and asked the man if he was serious. He smiled at me and nodded. His dingy skullcap almost fell from his head as he completed the movement. I asked him what I would get out of the deal if I won. He told me that he would be my slave for a day and if he won vice versa. I turned to my friends again. They sat there saying nothing with their faces painted with amusement. I turned to the foolish man and challenged him to an IQ test. After all, my IQ ranked me as a genius. I was positive that I would win. It was not possible for that street trash to succeed over me." Mr. Dole took a deep breath. He tried to refrain from the excitement he felt as he told his story.

"Do you need more water?" the doctor asked.

"Yes ma'am," Mr. Dole responded as he looked down at his shuffling bare feet. He observed how pale his feet were in comparison to his white pants. They nearly matched. He lifted his head in time for his lips to meet the paper cup held by the man in white. Mr. Dole drank quickly and the man in white returned to his post behind the doctor.

"Please continue," the doctor said as she leaned forward and placed her hands on her knees, stretching her back.

Mr. Dole leaned back in his chair and began.

"I invited the homeless fellow to my office. I could remember the faces of the people in my building as they watched me and my friends escort the foul smelling being through the lobby into the conference room. They all were flabbergasted!" Mr. Dole laughed quietly. "You should have seen their faces. All of them were so puzzled and confused by my colleagues and I and our strange company. Of course no one said a word. I was the boss. Who dared question the boss?" Mr. Dole shook his head, wet with sweat, and laughed aloud. After the salty liquid stung his eyes, he quickly disregarded his laughter and put on a straight face. "I ordered my secretary to print a couple of IQ tests off of the internet and bring them to me immediately. I offered the wastrel a breath mint and we all sat down."

"Did you care enough to ask his name?" the doctor asked.

"Yes, but I can't remember." A puzzled look crossed Mr. Dole's face. "It wasn't important." He shrugged his shoulders. "Anyhow, my secretary brought in the tests and a couple of pencils. My crony next to me offered to monitor the time for us." Mr. Dole paused. "To think of the entire affair, my companions and I were a little inebriated and looking for a good time and some poor fool provided us with the opportunity. We all loved to interact with lesser humans and show them how incompetent in life they were." Mr. Dole lowered his eyebrows and sighed. "The tramp and I finished the tests and I gave it back to my secretary to grade and return to us when she finished."

"Are you always so arrogant?" asked the doctor.

"What do you mean?" questioned Mr. Dole.

"Do you always belittle those who you consider less fortunate?" she said.

"I do no such thing. I call things as I see them. An idiot is an idiot. Is it my fault that I am honest?" Mr. Dole snapped.

The doctor raised her eyebrows to his response. She smiled and scribbled something on her notepad.

"Please continue," she said, not looking up from her notepad.

"We all sat in the conference room awaiting the return of my hired help. Stephanie finally came back into the room and gave one of my friends the results. I looked at the derelict and smiled an all knowing smile knowing that I was the better man by all means. The putrid smelling human did not acknowledge my contempt for him. He simply asked me to read the results. My buddy looked at the paper, twisted his face, stuck it back inside the manila envelope, and handed to me. I snatched it, offended by his look, and pulled the scores out. As I read the results, I could not believe my eyes. His scores were at least twenty points higher than mine! I was befuddled. My idiot of a secretary must have made a mistake. I wanted to crawl out of my skin. The dirty peon grinned at me and stood up. He walked across the room and stood in front of the picture frame window. He winked his misty gray eye at me and said, 'Let the games begin slave!' I yelled out that I was no one's slave and damned him to hell. He said, 'Are you breaking our bargain?' I told him hell yes and told him how I did not believe one minute that he was smarter than I was. He told me to have it my way and vanished right before our eyes."

Mr. Dole jumped from his chair. He paced the floor frantically. "Vanished I tell you!" he screamed. "I mean, puff and disappeared. Gone!" He stretched his eyes wide and stared into the eyes of the doctor. A single bead of sweat ran into his eye as he blinked repeatedly to free himself of the salty burn within his right eye.

"Do you need some tissue Mr. Dole?" The doctor asked in a very calm and slightly condescending tone.

"Yes," he said as he removed the crazed expression from his face and sat back down in his seat. The man in white walked over to Mr. Dole and wiped his dampened forehead and eye with a few facial tissues. Mr. Dole looked at the man in white and nodded his head. The man stood back behind the doctor.

"Better?" the doctor asked, smiling.

"Much, but why didn't you wipe my face the first time you noticed that my eyes were burning?" Mr. Dole mumbled under his breath while looking down at his ghastly feet.

"Please continue," said the doctor.

"After the man vanished, we all stood around amazed and scared stiff. What had I gotten myself into? We all went back to our offices and did not speak of the incident again. When time came for me to get off of work, I called home and asked my wife if she needed me to pick up anything." He paused and wrinkled his brows. "She asked me to pick up the strangest thing."

"What was that Mr. Dole?"

"She asked me to bring home seafood."

"How is that strange?" asked the doctor.

"My wife hates seafood. She thinks that shellfish looks like bugs."

"Understandable." The doctor nodded, permitting him to continue.

"I asked her why and she said that we had company and she wanted to fix something special. I asked her who was there and she just giggled and told me that she loved me and hung up the phone. I went to the store, picked up what I was instructed to pick up, and headed home. I was greeted by my beautiful wife. I put the food down and went into the living room. At first I was puzzled. I had no idea who was standing in front of me. As I looked closer, I realized that it was the strange homeless man and he had teeth! He was clean and exquisitely dressed; actually a very handsome man. He extended his hand out to me and called me Robert. I never told him my name and I know my wife did not. All who know me call me Zeke, short for Ezekiel, my middle name. I shook his hand and sat down. My wife kissed my cheek and led us both to the couch. She told me that Mr. Bush had asked her not to tell me that he was there. It was a surprise. Supposedly Mr. Bush was a big investor in my firm and he wanted to surprise me by coming over and talking about investing more money. All lies!" Mr. Dole snapped. "I gave my wife a false smile and kindly asked her to busy herself and leave us men to our business. She smiled her amazing smile, kissed me, and headed into the kitchen. After she had disappeared into the other side of the house, I ran over to Mr. Bush and tried to choke him."

Mr. Dole bolted from the chair but quickly sat down, realizing that his bound arms made it fruitless to demonstrate.

"The S.O.B. broke free from my grip and sat down as if nothing happened. He grinned at me with his big white teeth which reminded me of square bathroom tiles, all even and square like they were created in a factory; his grin forcing the anger to boil in me even more. I asked him what he wanted and he told me that I already knew. I was furious. This man had the gall to come into my house and invade my privacy. I told him to hell with the wager and to hell with him. He stared at me with cold eyes. He asked me if I was sure because the consequences would be substantially grave. I told the creepy bastard to get out and he placed his martini glass on the table, straightened his suit, and walked out of the door yelling a sweet goodbye to my wife. She came running to the door begging him not to leave. Frantically she pleaded. He declined the invitation, smiled at her, and walked out the door. A deep sadness fell over my wife. Her eyes became glossy and her shoulders dropped. I was in awe. How could she be so blue over a total stranger? What had he done to her? I took her in my arms; her golden hair fell lightly over my shoulder, and asked her what was wrong. She claimed that she had no idea and wept like a mourning mother." Mr. Dole's eyes became overweighed with tears. He looked at the doctor for understanding but she did or said nothing. His bottom lip trembled as his face drew into an awful frown. "Why the hell was she so distraught over this man?" Mr. Dole yelled into the doctor's face, spit sprinkling her jacket. The doctor held her hand up and the man in white handed her some tissue to wipe away the sticky saliva.

"Please continue Mr. Dole," the doctor instructed as she disposed of the tainted tissue.

"The next day I came home, my wife was still in a deep depression. She would not eat, sleep, or bathe. I was worried sick because my wife was an extremely meticulous woman. She sat on the edge of the bed in the same clothes from the day before. She looked awful. Her makeup was smeared. Her hair looked like a blonde mesh of barbwire. I tried to convince her to get into the shower but it was to no avail. She did not even blink. Tears ran down her cheeks as she sat in silence. This behavior continued for a week and I could not take it anymore. I had to find Mr. Bush. I jumped into my truck and I rode the streets day and night looking for that fiend. I wanted to know what he had done to my precious wife and what kind of spell he had put on her. Down the streets of Baton Rouge I sped looking for this man. I searched every street corner, restaurant, college campus, driveway, and swamp. I could not find him anywhere. I finally gave up and returned to my home. My spirits were down and I knew that my wife would be in the same predicament. I placed my key into the keyhole and opened the door. To my surprise, the whole house was filled with the aroma of freshly cooked seafood. I walked into the kitchen and there stood my wife dressed very eloquently in a powder blue chiffon gown that I bought her on last Valentine's Day. Her hair was in a French roll with a single golden ringlet falling in her face. Huge diamonds sparkled from her ears, fingers, and neck. They were the diamonds her grandmother had given her. Strangely she was cooking in this ballroom attire," Mr. Dole said. "Can you believe that she was cooking looking like that? Breathtaking! I walked over to her and kissed her shoulder. Her milky white skin felt so soft under my lips. I turned her to face me and stared into her perfectly made-up face. She smiled at me, kissed me passionately and told me that Mr.

Bush was there. Then, she turned around and finished cooking. I heard her humming a soft tune as I walked into the living room. And there he was sitting on my couch, drinking my wine, and bringing joy to my wife! With all the sanity I could muster, I asked him quietly what he did to my wife. He leaned his head to the side, insinuating that he did not hear me. I repeated myself and he leaned back on my couch and smiled. A wicked grin curled his lips as he looked at me. He asked me if I was ready to cooperate. I said never and he carelessly threw his hands up and said so be it. I told him to get out, not realizing my voice rang through the house. My wife ran into the room and begged Mr. Bush to stay. She said that she would die if he left. In anger, I snatched her away from him but she grappled for him and wailed louder and louder. I could not believe my eyes. She was all over this man weeping like a crazy woman. After taking all I could take, I grabbed her by the neck and tossed her out of the hallway. I did not realize my strength. My wife was a very small woman, under five feet and less than one hundred pounds. Mr. Bush laughed as I tried to help her but she pushed me away and ran into the kitchen. When she came out, she saw me trying to push Mr. Bush out of the door. He did not budge. He stood as if there was no force humanly possible that could move him. His clothes didn't even wrinkle under my touch. His cold eyes gleamed like fireflies. My wife yelled my name. I turned around to face her and she begged for me to not to make him leave. I ordered her to leave the room and let me handle this. She continued to beg but I told her that that hell spawn should not be allowed to step foot in our home again. From the folds of her dress she produced a knife. Showing no sign of sanity, she stabbed herself in the arm. The blood crawled around the blade. She did not even wince. Mr. Bush laughed. I cried out for her to stop. She then stabbed her legs. The scarlet liquid soiled her powder blue gown. I ran to her. Her hand shot upwards and with one swift movement, she slit her throat. I held her and cried hysterically. As I rocked her in my arms, her blood covered my clothes. Mr. Bush's cold smiling eyes invaded my flesh. A hurricane of anger brewed in my head. I dropped my wife and picked up the knife. Mr. Bush picked up the phone and dialed 911 and dropped the receiver to the floor. I pounced upon the icy-eyed demon and attempted to drive the knife through those haunting eyes. He fell under me and grabbed my wrist before the blade entered his face. He gave me a torturous grin and whispered the word arrogance in my ear and vanished. Moments later the police arrived at my house and found me covered in my wife's blood and with the life stealing blade in my hand. They put me in handcuffs like a common criminal. I was unfairly tried and deemed insane." Mr. Dole shook his head. "No one believes me!" he yelled. "No one believes me!"

The doctor looked at him, her ebony face damp with sweat because of the hot white light above her head. She leaned in toward Mr. Dole with the man in white leaning over her shoulder, both looking as if they were connected like Siamese twins. Mr. Dole looked into the icy cold eyes of the man in white and then noticed a wicked grin on the doctor's face.

"We believe you," the two said in unison, both morphing into Mr. Bush and then back into the doctor and her helper.

Mr. Dole bolted from his seat screaming for dear God as the hospital restrainers grabbed him and drug him back into his white padded room.

BLOODY MARY

Deep within the green countryside of Georgia, lived a very strange little girl. In appearance she was pale and unattractive and in mind she was simple. Because of her unkempt appearance, she was shunned by the other children on the nearby plantations. They thought of her as white trash and were cruel to her perpetually. Alone she was everyday, playing with sticks and stones because her parents could not afford any toys. The girl's name was Mary Documount. Sadness and despair rolled from her swollen eyes as often as the sun rose. Little did people realize that the lugubriousness of the little pariah's taunted soul would make her immortal.

The year was 1849. The Civil War had not yet begun and slavery was still flourishing in America. The day was crisp and bright and the warm air swirled around the small legs of a slave girl helping her mother pick cotton in the enormous plantation yard. A little slave girl, called Sissy, wandered very close to the small shanty house where the Documount family was permitted to live.

Mr. Documount was one of the overseers of Six Pines Plantation. He was poor but kind compared to other overseers. Especially Mr. Sanders, the head overseer, who was a cruel and malicious slave driver. He used any and every excuse possible to inflict pain on slaves. Once, a child picked up an apple core that Mr. Sanders had dropped and began to nibble on it. Mr. Sanders slapped the child so hard that the boy lost a tooth.

Generally, Mr. Documount dealt out very little punishment; only when he felt he had absolutely no choice. His employer regarded him as soft but kept him on because he required only minimum payment for the extraordinary work he did. The greedy plantation owner found his overseer's poverty mighty profitable. The savings granted the plantation owner the opportunity to live in excess and provided his wife with frequent dinner parties and his daughters with diamonds.

Behind a dingy screen door, Mary stood with her face pressed so hard against it that crisscross lines garnished her cheek. She saw Sissy and stepped out of the ragged door.

"Whatcha doin' out this far?" Mary asked with scorn in her voice. A crooked line crossed her forehead and her arms folded automatically.

"Isa jus pickin' cotton ova here. Isa don't mean no hum," the slave girl exclaimed. She had a narrow pretty face with enormous lashy eyes.

Mary walked closer and Sissy flinched.

"I aint gonna hurt ya. Get ova here and play wit me," Mary demanded. "My pa won't punish ya for not workin' cause I aint got no one else to play wit."

"Isa don't think that's a good idea. Massa might put the whip to me and ma," Sissy said, looking back over her shoulder at her concerned mother. Her eyes were as worried as Sissy's.

"I said get ova here fo' I get Mr. Sanders on ya anyhow!" Mary yelled, frustrated at Sissy's lack of enthusiasm. She thought that Sissy would be overjoyed with her invitation. Mary dropped her eyes to the ground. Instantly she felt guilty about the empty threat she had made. She would never tell Mr. Sanders on even the most insubordinate slave. He was much too barbarous. After all, she wanted Sissy to play with her out of choice not fear.

Sissy gave her bag to her mother with trembling hands and hesitantly walked over to Mary. Sissy's eyes darted rapidly from her mother to Mary. Nervous was too simple of an emotion to describe what she felt. It was more like dread. Fright mounted her back like a beast of burden. She knew no good would come from this.

Mary slowly walked over to a nearby mud puddle, dragging her feet making lines in the dirt. Her dingy dress was stained with the red clay of Georgia. Her face was freckled and her yellow gritty teeth made her look even more unkempt than a field hand working from dawn to dusk.

"Ova here gal," Mary spat. Her selfishness got the best of her.

Sissy scuffled over to the puddle and sat next to the strange smelling Mary.

"Yessam." She curtsied.

"Lessa make pies. Relax. I don't hate ya'll peoples. I am just as po' as you is. I only want a friend. Play wit' me please," Mary begged. "I'm so sorry fo' bein' mean ta ya. I would neva eva do anything ta hurt ya."

Mary looked Sissy deep into her eyes with quiet pleading. Mary was sincere.

Sissy didn't know how to react. Was this white girl trying to trick her? White folk were never to be trusted. Her mother told her that there was no good in them. Was Mary for real? Well, Sissy felt that she had no choice so she forced a smile and obliged. Minutes turned into hours and the little girls played and laughed.

Years passed and their friendship became as solid as oak. In time they began to love one another. Their friendship became the reason each of them drew breath in the morning and prayed before they slept at night. They became more than friends. They became sisters. Both began to blossom under the umbrella of friendship. Each learned how to accentuate their unique beauty and become young ladies of cleanliness and proper manners.

Sissy was used to being treated like trash. She was a slave and that was her life. Mary, however, never understood why she had to be called poor white trash and treated with contempt. She was a nice girl but no one would take the time to find out about her or Sissy. Soon she was known as a "nigga lover" which made her social status even lower than what it was before. Her father resented her friendship with Sissy but her mother loved Sissy like a daughter and she made it utterly clear that he was not to sabotage the relationship because Sissy was the only friend that Mary ever had.

Mr. Sanders belittled Mr. Documount on a daily basis for allowing his only child to befriend a slave. To Mr. Sanders, a slave was lower than a pig; an abomination unto the Lord. Mr. Documount often thought in response, "as if your evil spirit and cruel hand is a delight to God." Of course the slave women thought Mr. Sanders was an abomination. When left alone and unable to fight off his fleshy advances, he forced his way into their quarters at night and ravished them with animalistic violence and twisted aggression; all for his pleasure. It seemed as if there were more yellow slaves running around Six Pines with his blood flowing through their veins than there were rows of cotton.

When the time came for Mary to begin school, Mrs. Documount made Mary a white dress out of an eloquent old table cloth given to her by the master of the plantation. The cloth was made out of thick lacy cotton embroidered with small flowers and curly leaves. The dress was neatly made and Mary was very proud of it. With pride she put on her new shoes (which her pa diligently saved up for). Her mother tied a matching bow around Mary's thick wavy hair and Mary kissed her mother goodbye and made her way to school.

The road was long and dusty. It was lonely and quiet. Mary kicked pinecones for entertainment. In mid-kick she saw some kids around her age ahead of her and decided to catch up with them and attempt to make friends.

"How is ya'll doin' today?" Mary smiled showing her freshly cleaned teeth.

"Get away you poor white nigra lover!," a curly head blonde girl yelled into Mary's face as she pushed her to the ground.

"Leave me alone!" Mary cried.

"You filthy winch, I oughta kill you!" screamed a long haired boy while kicking her repeatedly.

Mary wept bitterly. Bruises appeared upon her flesh like magic. Blood covered her face like a mourning veil.

All six youngsters joined in on the beating. Sarah spit on Mary. Tommy stomped on her face. Jeanie kicked her in the ribs. Sam dropped to his knees and began punching Mary in the stomach until she vomited.

Milly scratched Mary on any bare spot she could find and the long haired boy, with a wicked glare in his eye, picked up a jagged rock.

"Let her go," Milly laughed a nervous laugh. "She aint worth the woopin' she just got."

"Please lemme go," Mary begged. "I only wanted ta be ya friend." She covered her head with her hands and balled up completely.

Tommy kicked her. Mary's hands fell free and the long haired boy leapt upon her with the rock held high over his head. He smiled. Mary screamed. He brought the rock down with every bit of power he possessed. He crushed Mary's skull. Blood oozed from her cranium like egg yoke.

"Josh!," yelled Sarah. "Look what you did! You killed her. What we gonna do now?"

"Nothin.' We didn't see this po nigga lovin' trash. Let's go wash up in that well over there before we get to school."

"But we can't leave her here! It aint right," Sarah squealed.

Milly started to cry. "I didn't really want to hurt her. I just wanted to push her around a bit."

"You're a murderer Josh!" Jeanie screamed.

"If you don't close that yapping hole, I will do you in," Josh threatened. "Let's go!"

The entire clan ran away from the scene.

Mary lay on the dirt road, limp and free of life. Her bloody body bled into the auburn soil. The sun dried the wound on her torn face. The wind shifted. An unearthly chill filled the air. An old root woman peeked out of the trees and a whisper was carried upon the wind calling Mary to awake. Her spirit separated from her scarlet damp body. Specter Mary's eyes popped open. She sat up. Her essence twisted and shifted like flickering light. Her face was paler than porcelain. Her hair was lily white with its edges dripping with blood. Her dress was now a scarlet gown and ivory chains draped around her transparent body. Raw to the bone with long black nails curving from them were her hands and feet. Her eyes glowed deep fiery red and endless tears of blood made trails down her cheeks. Out of her mouth bubbled blood and an eerie moan that would send chills down the back of Satan. Revenge would not let her tortured soul rest. Her name would bring wrath to the ones looking upon themselves and mentioning her.

The vengeful spirit looked upon her fallen human remains and howled in despair. She disappeared as the night crept in like a professional burglar.

Sissy had not seen Mary all day so she decided to leave her family, against her mother's desperate protests, and search for her companion. Sissy walked through the cotton fields, looking over her shoulder constantly praying that Mr. Sanders was in his home. Soon she arrived at the Documount's shack. She climbed the porch stairs and tiptoed to the window. Hiking up her skirt, she stepped up on a crate and peered into the window. Mary was nowhere to be seen. The Documounts looked worried and Mr. Documount was cursing and scrambling around the house looking for the spare lantern.

Sissy jumped from the crate and ran towards the dirt road. Out of her pocket she pulled a candle and match she took from the storehouse. She lit the candle and made her way down the dirt road. Darkness moved all around her. The hot wax scorched her ebony hand. She winced in pain but she had to find her crony. The candle began to burn low. Sissy decided to turn back when she tripped over something in the road. A foul smell invaded her nose. Flies swarmed around her. Something sticky was on her hands. She held the candle close to the ground and there she spied the mutilated body of Mary. A loud cry escaped her lungs and she dropped the candle and started to run. A bright beam of light shined in her face, blinding her temporarily. A couple of white men came trotting her way. She was covered in Mary's blood and the trees were too far to run to. That night she knew death would come. Her only wish was for it to be swift.

"Where ya goin' nigga?" a hideous looking white man asked as he spit a splash of tobacco colored saliva on the ground. "You tryin' to run away?"

"Nossa Massa Sanders." Sissy bowed her head.

"What's that all ova yo clothes gal?" another pale faced man roared, his bald head reflecting the light.

"Mary is dead. I found huh ova there. Somebody done killed huh. I didn't do it. I loved huh!"

Mary's father ran up the road and pushed through the men. He ran to the corpse. Tears raced down his face. His mouth turned downward and his hands quivered.

"You filthy nigga! You killed my Mary! You killed my Mary!" he howled.

Sissy disappeared that night. Her face was never seen alive again. When her body was discovered, she was naked and covered with deep gashes filled with salt. Sissy's mother mourned for her the rest of her days. Many nights she thought she heard the voice of her daughter whispering in her ear. Night after night she was overwhelmed with grief until her soul finally left to join her child.

*   *   *

Sarah walked into her eloquent plantation house. She skipped up her tall winding staircase and entered into her pink and white bedroom. She sat in front of her mahogany vanity and began to brush her curly blonde hair. Haunting thoughts of Mary infiltrated her mind. How did she know her name? Sarah was sure that Mary didn't tell her. She guessed it didn't matter. Sarah stood up, straightened her dress, and admired her reflection in the mirror.

"Who cares about that po white trash **MARY** anyway? Honorable white folks don't love darkies more than their own. She didn't deserve to live. **MARY** could have never been a respectable southerner anyhow. She is betta off where she is. To hell with **MARY**," Sarah exclaimed as she preened herself in the mirror. She smiled. That same smile vanished as easily as it came.

A figure took shape in her mirror. Sarah stumbled backwards not taking her eyes from the apparition. The bloody figure levitated in front of the frozen girl. Recognition stretched Sarah's eyes. A scream tried to make its way out of her mouth but before a sound could escape, Bloody Mary's chains had wrapped around Sarah's neck. The tortured spirit tightened the chain until Sarah's head separated from her body. A wicked smile spread across Mary's lips as blood spilled from the corners of her scarlet mouth. Mary disappeared into the depths of the mirror.

Mr. Taylor, Sarah's father, walked into her daughter's room the following morning. Terror filled him when his eyes fell upon his murdered daughter. The weeping man grabbed the headless body of his girl and held her close to him.

"Who did this to my Sarah?" he bellowed.

*   *   *

The bar in the city plaza was packed. Mr. Documount got up from his bar stool and walked out of the parlor headed to the outhouse. Heavily intoxicated, he staggered over to the wooden shed. The dizzy man saw a woman walking along the path adoring herself in a silver hand mirror. He wobbled over to her with his hand on his zipper. The woman screamed and threw her mirror at him. It hit him in the head and he fell to the ground. He picked up the looking glass and looked at the mess he had become. He had gone from an honorable husband to a dizzy drunk.

"Oh **MARY**, look at what I have become. Why did that gal kill my **MARY**? **MARY**, why did ya have ta go?" the old man cried as he stared at his reflection. Red mist formed in the mirror and twisted its way out in tiny wisps. Mr. Documount threw the mirror down and ran for the outhouse. The mist morphed into Bloody Mary and the she-demon blocked her father's path.

"Who are you?" His inebriated eyes squinted. "Mary is that you?"

Mary inserted her talon like fingernails into her father's temples. She pressed until both of her fingers vanished into each side of his head. The old man's dead body dangled between her hands and she removed her bony fingers and let his limp body fall to the ground. Blood poured from the holes in his head like strawberry syrup oozing from an open bottle. Bloody Mary was satisfied. Her chains became lighter. Mary hovered over the hand mirror. Her misty spirit swirled and faded into the looking glass.

*   *   *

The two men who aided Mary's father in Sissy's murder were walking down the street telling lewd jokes and chewing tobacco. The uglier of the two, Mr. Sanders, pulled out his pocket knife and proceeded to whittle away on a small block of wood that he had in his pocket.

Mr. Zacket paid little attention to his friend's carving until a wood chip flew into his eye.

"Ya darn fool! Look whatcha did. Ya hit me straight in the eye. Gimme yo knife so I can see myself," the bald man shouted as he snatched the shiny blade from his companion. He held the knife to his face to see his refection and commenced to finding the offending object.

"It's a shame what happened to Ned Documount's gal Mary isn't it?" Mr. Sanders asked his friend.

Zacket was steady picking his eye. "Yeah **MARY** was a strange gal. Even though she was a worthless thang, that nigga had no right to be always clinging to her, acting like she was the same as that white gal, like she was equal or somethin'. I know that nigga didn't kill **MARY**. She was her friend but I say niggas and white folks should never be friends. She deserved the killin' she got." He paused, his hangdog face lined with a tiny bit of guilt. "Somebody had to pay for po **MARY**'s death," the bald man said in a sad justifying tone.

While holding the blade close to his eye, Zacket realized that the blade was turning red. The handle became so hot that he threw the weapon to the ground. The knife rose into the air; the tip pointed towards the ground. Blood dripped from the knife, each drop growing grotesquely bigger with each fall until a bloody body was formed.

The men tried to run but a low moaning froze them in their steps. They lost all control of their bodies. They knew that they would soon go the way of the dodo.

Blood Mary floated over to the men. She wrapped one of her chains around Zacket. The chain burned through his flesh until only blood, smoke, and bone was left.

Sanders stood next to the gruesome display, straining to cry. Mary took both of his arms and ripped them from their sockets. Then she took his knife and split is chest in half. All the while she sang an eerie tune whose pitch became higher and higher until their bodies exploded in a thousand pieces. Bloody Mary dissolved into the air, a red mist floating on the breeze.

*   *   *

Tommy Sims sat outside of his grandmother's house, staring into her crystal clear pond. He counted the fish that swam around and tried to feed the turtles and nearby frogs.   They were very disinterested. Guilt claimed his conscious and he thought about the murder of Mary. He could see her crushed skull so vividly. Tears flowed from his baby blue eyes as he examined his refection in the transparent pond.

"Forgive me **MARY**. I didn't mean for you to die. I didn't kill you, **MARY**. I don't know if your name is **MARY** but somehow that name seems to fit you. Forgive me. I should have stopped him. We should have left you alone in the first place. Forgive me," the boy cried as his tears made ripples in the now scarlet pond. He wiped his eyes in disbelief. The pond was bright red. He leaned closer when a head came out of the water and arms grabbed his head and pulled it under. Bubbles besieged the surface of the water as his muffled screams and flailing arms succumbed to the silence of death.   Bloody Mary released him, kissing his blue cheek, and uttered, "I forgive you."

*   *   *

The Foster house was filled with party guests.   Music swam through the air like tropical fish. Jeanie loved her parent's parties. She loved the way her father's guests all fawned over her and made her feel like pure royalty.

Jeanie ran into her mother's room to look in the great mirror to ensure that she was still looking as perfect as possible. The mirror took over an entire wall. Jeanie posed and smiled at how she looked in her new party dress. The pale green material complimented her eyes and she just loved the way her bosom looked in the off the shoulder ruffles. She spun around for a rear view when she thought she saw someone pass the door. Jeanie dropped her ruffled skirt over her white petticoat and stuck her head out of the door. There was no one in the hall.

"**MARY**, is that you?" she asked. She was referring to her cousin Marilee. "**MARY**, answer me this minute!" Jeanie demanded, placing her hands upon her hips. "**MARY**, stop playing games. I know I saw you," she huffed. A chill snaked down her arms. "I will not let that silly thing worry me," she tried to convince herself and made her way back to the mirror.

Jeanie was somehow oblivious to the entity that stood behind her. Bloody Mary grabbed the girl by the back of her neck and flung her into a nearby wall. Mary forced

Jeanie's mouth open wide with her dark claws and covered the girl's mouth with her own. Jeanie tried to break free but Mary's grip was too solid. Jeanie punched and kicked but her limbs passed through Mary's body like birds pass through clouds. Blood poured from Mary's mouth, filling the girl's mouth with scarlet slime until she choked on the overabundance of liquid. Mary dropped Jeanie's dead body to the floor and vanished into the mirror.

"Jeanie," Marilee called down the hall, looking for her cousin. "Your pa is looking for you. He wants to dance with his favorite girl," she said while sticking her head in each door as she passed through the hall. Marilee stuck her head into her aunt's room and saw Jeanie lying on the bed with her mouth ajar and her face covered in blood. An ear piercing scream flooded the mansion.

*   *   *

Sam and Milly sat in the dining hall of the Parker Plantation. The young couple sat at the table sipping peach rum punch out of a sterling silver punch bowl. They took sips from the edge of the bowl so that Mrs. Parker, Sam's mother, would not realize that they were drinking her party punch. They infuriated the house slave, Big Liza, because she was constantly refilling the vanishing punch.

The youngsters giggled and kissed each other as they stole sips every time Big Liza left the room grumbling under her breath. Seconds turned into minutes and minutes became uncountable. Their jolly mood dissolved into drunken lightheadedness. Sam checked his bloodshot eyes in the side of the bowl. An evil grin curled the left side of his lips.

"Are my eyes as red as **MARY**'s bloody head after we did her in?" the intoxicated boy asked while laughing. The visual of blood sent a strange thrill down his spine. "I bet God didn't even let that trashy heifer into heaven. What good would **MARY** be to Him but to empty the slop jar?" he laughed. "Could you imagine angel poop?" Sam could hardly contain his laughter. His eyes never left the bowl. He was fascinated by the way his eyes danced. "You know what? If **MARY** was still alive, I would beat her again," the stupid boy roared with drunken amusement. Milly joined in with high pitched giggles. Little did they know that the end of all things was upon them.

"Kill me," a low groan rang in their ears. "Kill me," it resounded louder. Bloody Mary's face appeared on the side of the bowl in front of Sam. He fell out of his chair.

"I must be drunk as hell," he chuckled. The smile left his face when he saw the stricken look in Milly's eyes.

Mary exited the shiny surface and floated above Sam. A bloodcurdling sound came from her mouth and the two were instantly paralyzed and rendered mute. Their eyes stretched in horror. Bloody Mary forced them face down on the floor and whipped them with her chains until their very flesh folded from their bones and fell to the hard wood floor like paper. Milly and Sam perished in ultimate pain under the heavy chains of Mary. The vengeful spirit rose above the punch bowl and dissolved into the peach colored liquid without a trace.

*   *   *

Joshua Matthews walked home alone as the afternoon morphed into evening. He decided to take a short cut by the creek next to the road where he had maliciously murdered Mary. The sun hung its head low and a chill was in the air. Josh walked by the banks of the creek, throwing pebbles into the water.

Shadows clouded his mind. He could have sworn that he heard a voice calling him. Voices called him often. He could hear them daring him to do their bidding. The long haired boy threw himself down on a rock and stared at his reflection in the pale green creek water.

"Why did you do it?" he asked himself.

"**MARY** deserved it!" he answered himself. "She was nobody."

"You still had no right to kill **MARY**!" he yelled at himself.

"Damn **MARY**! To hell with her worthless soul!" he screamed into the water.

"To hell with you!" a voice not of his own answered.

Josh could not believe his ears. He looked around but he saw no one. He looked back into the water. Nothing. He washed his face in the creek water when he felt a sharp pain in his back. A squeal fell from his lips. He looked back and saw the girl he murdered with a jagged stone in her hand. Bloody Mary took the stone and crushed his hands and feet. He bellowed in pain and begged for mercy. He called for God but God did not answer. She took the stone that stole her life and with the force of a thousand demons, she crushed his dome into infinite fragments.

Bloody Mary's mission was complete. The chains draping her fell to the earth and were no more. Her blood tears evaporated. Her hair regained its natural appearance and her dress was as clean and white as the day her mother made it. A bright light appeared before her. Out of the light emerged Sissy with her arms wide open. Mary ran into her best friend's arms and they faded into the dusk.

Legend says that Mary's soul still roams the earth looking for the ancestors of the people who murdered her and Sissy. Evil awakes her from her rest every twenty-five years to do its murderous bidding. The elders say that they can hear her eerie moaning late at night when foolish youngsters look at their refection and call her name, Bloody Mary, thrice. Sightings of her are still reported today. Be careful not to call upon her name, you may be an ancestor.

CRUMBLING

Right before my eyes, I see the world changing; a great metamorphosis into something deathly horrid and obscene. Sad, sad like a single tear in a widow's eye or like the loss of a playoff game by one point. Everything is crumbing, becoming nothingness in my sight. No hope. No one to save it. All because....

This morning the world was a beautiful place. The sun shined a little brighter. The moon smiled upon the earth as it brought in the tides. My life was wonderful. I had a woman who loved me. I was the carefree head of my bank's department. Yesterday my son gave me the best father's day gift that I ever had. I was sitting on top of the world, smoking a cigar with my feet crossed and my head held high. Then, Misery walked into my life.

You see, Misery loves company. She was the finest woman on this side of the Mississippi. She was tall like pine, black like crow, and talked smoother than a radio. I tell you, that girl had legs up to her eyebrows and a figure that put an hourglass to shame. You know the kind of girl; the kind that is a sight to look at but a sin to have. Every heterosexual man and confused female was stunned by her beauty. What was I to do? My wife was a beautiful woman but like I said, Misery loves company.

Well to get to the point, I was sitting in my office when my secretary buzzed my phone. I picked up and she said that my 3:15 appointment was waiting for me. The tone of her voice sounded funny as if it had an element of warning me about my potential client. Conscience never steered my wrong. I told Conscience to send her in. I straightened up my suit, brushed my beard, and took my feet off of the table. My door swung open and in walked Misery. The girl had on a skirt around her neck and a shirt around her forehead. I took a deep breath and attempted to ignore her God given assets. And I may say that I thank God everyday for creatures like this. I took another breath and asked her to sit down. She sat in the chair in front of me and crossed those long curvy legs of hers. She had to be at least six feet tall in those heels. She had light gray eyes and a hellish smile. She wore a leather skirt in the dead of summer. It was so tight that I could see the seam print on her thigh every time she moved. Her shirt was sheer with two pockets in front hiding her breasts. Thank goodness! I looked away and sat down again.

"What may I help you with, Miss..." I looked at her file. "Miss Misery Wilruinyurlife? I am Soweak Lameassman. It is a pleasure to meet you." I smiled and shook her hand. "What an interesting name."

"My mother gave it to me. She always told me that I was a little devil." Misery laughed, showing those pearly white teeth and her dark purple gums. She had the kind of laugh that made my skin crawl. You know the kind that is deep and soul grabbing; a mixture between the Wicked Witch of the West and the little girl in *The Exorcist.*

"I need a loan in the amount of $75,000," she said as she flashed me with those glistening white teeth. They were whiter than baby powder in a snow storm.

"Miss Wilruinyurlife, that is a lot of money. What do you have as collateral? Do you own a home, land, anything?"

"No."

I laughed. "We cannot help you ma'am. It was nice talking to you." I looked into her eyes and froze like ice.

"Yes you can," she whispered. Misery came closer to me, those gray eyes not blinking once. I was helpless. Before I could blink, I was naked. She was naked. We both were naked. We were working like the chain gang on a hot summer day, like a single mother before quitting time, like an old Chevy pushed to the limit. We were working.

After a few moments, I approved her for a loan, gave her the keys to my car, and was wondering how in the hell was I going to explain this to my wonderful wife.

I was startled by a knock on the door.

"Who is it?" I asked nervously.

Misery quickly dressed herself, winked at me and tossed me my car keys.

"Thanks but I already have a car." She smiled, winked, and vanished like an apparition. I mean gone in a twinkling of an eye. Scared the mess out of me! I figured I was dreaming until Conscience walked in. Her eyes laced with disgust and severe disapproval.

"Where have you been?" I asked, afraid that she may have overheard something.

Guilt was all over my face and not to mention that my jacket was thrown on my desk, my shirt buttons missing, and me sitting in the middle of the floor may have looked a bit incriminating.

"I have been here like always. I hope that you know what you are doing. You should've picked up when I first heard the racket in here and rang your phone to stop you from selling your soul. You should've listened to me, Soweak. I tried to warn you about her. Maybe you wouldn't be in so much trouble," Conscience said, biting her lip.

"Like always you are right," I whined.

She clocked out for the evening and left me to wallow in my own mess.

I sat there feeling stupider than ever with scratches on my back, lipstick on my shirt, and the funk of Misery all over my body. What am I to do? The phone rang.

"Hello," I said.

"Hey baby, it's me, Loyalty. I missed you. When are you coming home?"

Dang, it's the wife!

"I'll be home in a little while baby. I have a meeting. I should be there in a couple of hours."

"Great! I have a surprise for you. I hope you feel sexy tonight!" she squealed and hung up the phone.

I had to clean up. I went to the restroom and washed up. I took off of my shirt and grabbed one of the ones off of the hanger that I was going to have Conscience take to the cleaners.

There was nothing that I could do about the scratches though. I left the office and jumped into my car. I stopped by the florist and bought Loyalty some flowers. I had to find a way to avoid undressing in front of her tonight. I pulled into the driveway and Loyalty was at the door before I could get out of the car.

"Hey baby!" She ran to me and kissed my lips. Her face cringed. "What have you been eating? Your breath smells funny."

"I had a miserable lunch." I answered, dying inside. Why did I have to be so weak?

We walked inside of the house and there were lit candles everywhere. The smell of perfume was in the air. A pallet was on the floor composed of satin sheets and rose petals. After observing all of this, I also observed that my loyal wife was a naked as a jay bird. Stunned was an understatement for what I was. I could not undress! The scratches on my back would incriminate me.

"Baby…" I tried to give her the flowers. She dropped them to the floor while kissing me wildly. I could not say a word. She was stripping me like a hoodlum strips a car on a deserted street. I tried to resist but the animal in me succumbed to her advances.

She saw a scratch.

"What is that?" Loyalty asked and pulled up my shirt before I could stop her. "What is the meaning of this, Soweak?" she screamed. Tears of pain and anger raced down her cheeks.

She slapped me every time she saw a new mark. The next thing I knew, I was standing outside on the lawn watching my clothes being burned and holding the bleeding gash on the side of my head inflicted by my ex-wife's shoe.

My boss did not approve of me giving away such an absurd amount of money to someone who did not qualify and he wanted to speak to me as soon as possible. He never spoke to anyone unless he is going to fire or promote them and I did not see a promotion in the near future.

My son would not talk to me. He called me a dirty dog and hated me for hurting his mom.

Loyalty and Conscience were so right. Misery Wilruinyurlife ruined my life and now I, Soweak, am weak and alone. I find myself on the way to the office with my life crumbling; crumbling like a hard cookie stepped on, like the seventh seal under the strength of the Lamb, like a piece of day old toast squeezed in my palm. Crumbling, impossible to put together again.

DISCONNECTED

Her tears were like silver icicles stabbing into her trembling cheeks as she wept in the cold night air. The moon was full and the sky was clear. Silence rang loudly. Genaline stood on her balcony sobbing hysterically. Her short black hair fell into her face and stuck to her damp cheeks while her small white hands balled into air tight fists swinging through the biting air. Anger hugged her tightly. Her husband had left her. Their marriage was perfect. How could such a thing occur? Their marriage was secure. It was to never end. Now she had to end it all. She could not dream of living without Harold. Genaline placed her delicate foot upon the banister as her arms lifted her body upward. She came to a standing position, balancing herself upon the rail, the air ripping across her quaking body. The cold was biting through her nightgown like the fangs of a hungry vampire.

"Harold, I will never have peace because if you!"

Genaline leapt from the balcony in a perfect diver's position, arms spread eagle and feet pressed together. Moments later, her bloodied body lay on the concrete in a lifeless, haggard, crimson lump of flesh. The police arrived and directed the gape mouth crowd away from the tragic scene.

Around five o'clock Tuesday morning when Harold received the news of Genaline's death, he was devastated. He never thought that she would take their separation that hard. Not hard enough to die over. He knew that he was to blame.

Harold removed his arm from under his nude mistress Fatima's body. His eyes were red and bagged. He decided that he needed a drink so he pulled the covers away from his pale pink skin and sat up in bed. With fumbling fingers, he blindly searched for his robe at the foot of the bed. He pulled the silk robe over his shoulders and stood up quickly. The movement awakened Fatima.

"What's wrong honey?" the golden skinned woman asked. "Are you okay?"

"Yeah," Harold said as he ran his hands through his curly blonde hair. "I'm just fine," he lied.

Harold walked out of the bedroom and into the dining room. He ran his fingers across the wall trying to find the light switch. A wet spot on the wall startled him. He jerked his hand away and wiped it on his beige robe. Reluctantly, he placed his hand back on the wall; this time finding the light switch. Harold shuffled over to the bar and fixed himself a scotch and soda. He drank the first glass down quickly and then refilled. Sitting on a large square stool, he fingered the leather bar top.

"Why Genaline? Why kill yourself?" he bent his head and groaned. He took a swig of the liquor and slammed the crystal glass down hard.

"You left me," a voice cried softly.

Harold leapt from to his feet, knocking the stool to the floor. His eyes searched the room. Goose pimples traveled up his arms. There was no one there. He must have imagined it. Impulsively, he grabbed his drink and downed the whole glass in one gulp. With trembling hands, he put the glass down and walked back into the bedroom.

Fatima's peculiar eyes raped him.

"What's that on your robe?" she asked while pointing.

Harold looked down and saw what looked like blood on his robe.

"Where did that come from?" Fatima asked with worry in her stretched eyes and fear at the tip of her tongue. She sat up in bed and fiddled with the top sheet.

"I don't know," he replied. "I don't know." His heart was beating a mile a minute in his chest. Harold wanted to tell Fatima what he thought he heard but she was not a confidant. Her only good qualities were her figure and sexual prowess. In bed, she was a Persian goddess. She had the ability to make him see past all her shortcomings and think of nothing more than the pleasure she gave. Her face was average at best and her compassion and concern for others was even lower. She was his match: shallow, materialistic, and selfish.

"What do you mean you don't know?" Fatima snapped.

"I don't know," he grumbled.

Harold climbed into the bed next to his seething mistress and the moon and the stars shined on the first night.

The alarm clock rang and Harold opened his eyes to the emptiness of his bedroom. An important meeting with a partner in his law firm was scheduled that morning so he had to get dressed quickly. Harold promptly got out of bed and jumped into the shower. Exiting the bathroom, the faint aroma of bacon and pancakes filled his nose. By the time he dried off and wrapped his towel around his waist, Fatima brushed past him and slammed the bathroom door in his face. He heard the shower water beat against the tub so he shrugged his shoulders and dressed quickly. Fatima would be finished with her daily pout by the time he got back home so he decided to leave her be.

As Harold ate his breakfast, he felt ice cold hands massage his muscular back. He smiled and leaned his head to the side. Soft nibbling tickled his neck and a cold wet tongue filled his ear. The advance was not pleasurable because of the coolness but he decided not to aggravate Fatima anymore than he had already.

"Why don't you do this more often? I love it when you touch me like this," he whispered

"Because you left me."

Harold jumped to his feet. There was no one there. He ran his fingers through his hair and placed his hand on his hip, looking around again. Still, there was no one there. He ran into the bathroom and swung the door open with so much force that Fatima almost jumped out of her skin.

"What the hell!" Fatima screamed. "What are you doing Harold?"

Harold's face went pale. Was he going mad? What had just happened in the dining room? He looked into Fatima's soft face and closed the door in front of him. He could hear her yelling and swearing on the other end of the door but he walked to the closet, grabbed his coat, left the house, and burned rubber on the way to work.

The sun shined bright and the clouds were visible on the first morning.

"Why are you late Harold?" John Cox yelled into his partner's face. Spit sprinkled Harold's cheeks. "You were supposed to be here a half an hour ago!"

Cox grabbed Harold's arm with his right hand and Harold's brief case with his left. He literally drug Harold into the conference room.

In the middle of the room sat a mammoth round table occupied by five bald pink men, two brown women, a golden man, three blue men, and two pale women. With annoyed faces, they eyeballed the late comers. A tall pink man stood up at the end of the table and waved his hand to motion Harold and John (his partner) to have a seat. The two men sat down and the meeting began.

Minutes turned into hours as the President of the firm lectured on. The secretary entered the room and poured fresh glasses of water and cups of steaming coffee.

When Mrs. Langly, the secretary, came to Harold, she leaned forward and poured him a cup of coffee. On her finger, it looked like his late wife's wedding ring. He looked into her face and he saw Genaline. Harold jumped to his feet and spilled the hot coffee all over his lap. The secretary ran and grabbed a napkin and tried to wipe the hot liquid from Harold's lap. He shoved her away. She stumbled backwards but quickly regained her footing.

"Who are you?" he screamed.

"Elizabeth Langly," she answered with a trembling voice. Her eyes rimmed with tears and her breath came in big gulps.

Harold looked into Mrs. Langly's face and his grimace disappeared. She was not Genaline. His imagination had gotten the best of him and now he had assaulted the secretary in front of the entire firm.

"I am sorry. Please forgive me. I have been under a lot of stress lately. I thought that you were someone else. If your offer is still extended, I would like your help," Harold apologized as he gestured for her to come near him.

As Mrs. Langly bent down to wipe his suit and chair, she whispered, "Why did you leave me?"

Harold pushed her to the floor and ran from the room. The entire conference room sat amazed on the first afternoon.

"He's mad I tell you. Plain insane!" yelled Gordon Bandoff, the president of the firm Bandoff, Cox, Wheeler & Bunden LLC.

"Bunden embarrassed me in front of the staff. He needs to see a doctor or he will be unemployed soon. I understand that a tragedy occurred in his life but his actions were inexcusable. We are lucky if Elizabeth doesn't sue. Do you hear me Cox? You better talk to Harold and do it soon!" The old wrinkled man stormed out of Cox's office, slamming the door so hard that the windows trembled.

Cox drummed his fingers on the desk. He scratched his head wildly and leaned back in his chair. How could he tell Harold that everyone thinks he is psychotic? John Cox reached across his metal desk and picked up the phone and quickly dialed Harold's number. The answering machine came on.

"Harold, this is John. We need to talk. Call me at work as soon as possible and maybe we can meet over dinner tonight or breakfast tomorrow. Goodbye." Cox hung up the phone.

Harold sat in his new car with his head pressed against the steering wheel. The lights in the parking deck casted him in shadow, creating a menacing look about his face. He ran his fingers through his curly blond hair and let out a humongous sigh. He started the engine and maneuvered his way out of the parking lot. While pulling through the exit gate, he opened his glove compartment to fish out a cigarette. A stack of his wedding pictures fell to the floor, carpeting the passenger side completely.

"How did this get in there?" he mumbled.

Harold picked up the pictures and flipped through them. He and Genaline were so happy then. She was so beautiful with the most incredible smile in the world. Her short black hair felt like silk and he loved the way it contrasted with her sun tanned skin.

"I used to love her," he said to himself as he continued to flip through the pictures. He found a picture of Fatima. Suddenly he didn't know how to feel. He adored Fatima's sexy body and her doe eyes. "I couldn't help myself." A devilish grin wrinkled his pink mouth.

"You couldn't help me either," a voice whispered in his ear from behind.

Harold jumped out of his skin. He swung around and frantically searched his back seat. Nothing was there. Harold stepped on the gas and sped out into the street, refusing to let up until he was stopped by a small traffic jam. Dark clouds covered the heavens and thunder sounded on the first evening.

The smell of fresh fried fish permeated Harold's house. He hung his coat on the rack and shuffled into the kitchen. Fatima stood in front of the stove with her back to Harold. She wore nothing but panties and an apron. The emotionally shaken man slowly made his way to his girlfriend and wrapped his arms around her so tight that her ribs ached.

"I'm going insane," he cried.

Fatima turned around to face him. She took her apron and whipped his tears away and asked, "What's wrong sweetie?"

"Genaline," he whimpered. "She haunts me! It is my fault that she died."

"Nonsense. She died because she was weak. You had nothing to do with her death. Disconnect yourself from it," she said; her middle eastern accent thick.

Harold looked deep into Fatima's eyes. "I was disconnected and that disconnection caused her death! She was such a good wife and I treated her like a dog."

"Harold, do you regret leaving her for me?" Fatima searched his face.

"No."

"Do you love me?" she asked.

"Yeah," he mumbled.

"Do you really think you killed her?"

"No, but..."

"But nothing. Don't worry. I feel bad about her death too but there is nothing we can do about it now. Why feel guilty for no reason? We did not mean to hurt her. We could not control our hearts," Fatima said as she caressed his chin. "Let her soul rest. Wipe her from your thoughts, okay."

"Okay." Harold dropped his head.

Fatima put her arms around him and held him. Trying to offer comfort the best way she knew how, she passionately kissed his invisible lips and ran her fingers through his golden hair letting her fingers fall to his shoulders then to his chest then to his inner thigh.

A smile curled Harold's lips. He buried his head in her breast and savored the feel of her exploring hands. The smell of burnt fish hit their noses like a fist.

"Oh my goodness!" Fatima screamed as she pushed Harold to the side and tried to put the grease fire out.

Harold laughed and walked out of the kitchen and into the bedroom. He fell across the bed and let out a sigh of relief. His eyes closed and he allowed his muscles to completely relax into the pillow top mattress. The warmth of the room was suddenly interrupted by a cold breeze. Harold crawled out of the bed and groggily went to the window to close it but it was shut and locked. He shook off the chill and made his way to the nightstand. He sat on the side of the bed and pushed the play button on his answering machine.

The machine began to play back his messages.

BEEP

"Harold, this is mom. Sorry to hear about Genaline. Are you alright?"

BEEP

"Fatima, this is Cher. Call me!"

BEEP

"Fatima, I've been trying to get in touch with you. Call me. This is Sharonda."

BEEP

"Harold, this is John. We need to talk. Call me as soon as you get this message. Maybe we can do dinner tonight or breakfast in the morning. Goodbye."

BEEP

"Harold, why did you leave me?"

Harold jumped to his feet. Sweat ran from his brow. His heart banged against his chest. He ran into the kitchen and grabbed Fatima's arm. He pulled her into the bedroom.

"Listen!" he yelled as he pushed the red button on the answering machine. The last message was gone. The voice of Genaline was gone.

"Listen to what?" Fatima squealed as she jerked her arm away.

Tears ran from Harold's face in streams of silver. His pink face turned bright red as he dropped to the bed and wept like a newborn baby.

Fatima shook her head. She was disgusted by his blubbering. "Weak!" she squealed and walked out of the room.

His tears flowed like mighty streams on the second night.

The night was long but with the certainty of time, the morning conquered the darkness and shed its light.

Harold woke a couple hours earlier than usual. His eyes were still red and puffy. Sitting up slowly, he picked up the telephone and dialed John's number.

"Hello," John's muffled voice answered.

"Sorry to wake you," Harold lied. "Let's have breakfast."

"Okay," John cleared his throat. "Meet me at Eva's at 8 o'clock. I'll be on time. You do the same."

"Will do," said Harold then hung up the phone. He dressed himself in an olive green three piece suit then walked into the bathroom to mousse his hair. Blond curls circled his fingers as he finger combed his hair. The shower curtain moved in the corner of his eye. He turned to face it and a feminine shadow materialized and dematerialized instantly. Snatching the curtain open, he saw nothing. He faced the mirror again and the shower curtain opened behind him. A pale hand rested within the folds. He spun around once more to find emptiness. The curtain was open.

"I'm losing my mind," he whispered as he turned back to the mirror to finish grooming. This time Genaline was standing right behind him wearing the same nightgown she had died in. Harold bolted from the bathroom, tripping twice but keeping his speed. He grabbed his coat and headed for the front door. With one foot out of the car, he cranked the engine and flew out of the driveway. Red lights were ignored as he zoomed though the intersections. Soon a cop was hot on his tail.

"Damn!" Harold growled as he pulled over and pulled his license out of his wallet. A short bald Asian cop walked to Harold's car door.

"License and registration, sir."

Harold gave it to him.

"Why were you speeding?" asked the officer.

"I'm running late for a business meeting. I didn't realize my speed." Harold swallowed hard. "I'm very sorry."

"Is your business meeting more important than the safety of all the people you could have killed?" the cop asked while writing a ticket.

"No sir," Harold answered.

"Well, why were you speeding?"

Harold furrowed his brow. "I told you sir."

"That's not good enough. I should take you to jail!" the police officer threatened.

"For what? I wasn't going that much over the speed limit. Give me a ticket and let me go! This is harassment! I'm a lawyer. I know my rights!" Harold barked. His face was beet red and he held out his hand for his license.

"I don't care who you are!" the cop barked back.

"Do as you wish!" Harold growled.

The police officer took Harold's license and wrote him a ticket. Harold snatched the ticket and sped away.

"You freakin' prick!" the cop yelled after him.

Harold arrived at Eva's Restaurant about thirty minutes late. John was sitting by the entrance tapping the face of his watch and shaking his head.

"Where have you been? You knew we had a meeting at 8. It's 9:15! I really need to talk to you," John grumbled.

"I got a ticket, besides; the meeting was scheduled for 8:45."

"It happens," John sighed as he waved for Harold to follow him. "You look like hell; pale as a ghost."

"Humph, ghost...," Harold whispered with an uneasy look in his eyes.

John shook his head and dropped his ebony hand onto Harold's shoulder. His heavy paw directed Harold to the table.

The men sat down and picked up menus. Harold glanced at it momentarily then looked across the table.

"What's up?" he asked, as calm as he could, trying to shake the eerie memories of seeing his dead wife in his bathroom earlier.

John put down his menu and folded his big hands together. He cleared his throat and said, "Well, you know you looked really foolish at the meeting yesterday. The secretary wasn't pleased by your behavior and Bandoff was furious. After you left, he called me into his office." John waved for the waitress to come near. He looked into her light brown eyes and said, "I'm ready to order."

"What will you have sir?" the waitress asked.

"Bacon, grits, eggs, and a hot buttermilk biscuit. He will have the same with two large orange juices please," John ordered and smiled as he watched the pretty young waitress walk away.

Harold rolled his eyes and straightened his tie.

"I think I could've ordered for myself," he grumbled.

"No time!" John tapped the face of his watch. "As I was saying, Bandoff was pissed. He wants you to see a doctor." John tapped his temple. "A head doctor."

"Why?" Harold frowned.

"Because you behaved like a lunatic!" John howled.

"John, do you think I need a doctor?"

"I think you need Jesus," John laughed.

"What if I refuse?" Harold crossed his arms.

John looked Harold in the eye and said, "Then you'll be selling encyclopedias!"

Harold shook his head and asked, "Bandoff said that?"

"I'm being nicer," John replied as he sat back in his seat and waited for his breakfast.

Anxiety burdened Harold's heart on the third morning.

All day the office was unusually quiet. Time moved at snail pace and Harold worked at his desk at an even slower rate. Babyface serenaded him as he shifted through the endless files on his desk. His secretary rang his phone.

"Yes Melonie?"

"Miss Vahid is on line one," the secretary replied.

"Put her through."

The line transferred and a soft voice pulsated through the speaker.

"Hey baby!"

"Hi Fatima," Harold said in a monotone voice. "What do you want?"

Fatima's voice changed from happy to annoyed. "Excuse me for calling!" she screeched.

"I didn't mean it that way baby. I'm just sort of busy."

"It's okay," she whined. "Is that Babyface playing in the background?"

"Yeah," he mumbled.

"I must be rubbing off on you. In a little while, you're gonna be a 2Pac fan." She laughed.

"Whatever!" he half heartedly chuckled. "Seriously, what's up?"

"Well, it's almost lunchtime and I just wanted to know if I could come and take you out? With your money of course," she giggled.

"Sure. Be here at 1 o'clock," he replied. "Bye."

"Bye."

Harold hung up the phone and another call came through.

"Melonie, who is it?"

"She won't tell me," Melonie answered.

"It's probably one of the partners. Put her through," Harold hissed.

The line transferred.

"Why did you leave me Harold? I loved you! You killed me and I'm going to kill you!"

Harold threw the phone across the room. Tears flooded his eyes. His face turned crimson. With one fierce sweep, everything on his desk went crashing to the floor. Harold punched his wall until Melonie, his secretary, and his partners John and Shannon came rushing into his office. Instantly he stopped, a complete emotional wreck, and looked helplessly at them.

"Harold," Shannon walked cautiously towards him. "I think you need to go home."

John stepped in front of Shannon and said, "No one asked you what you thought." He turned to Harold and said, "Go do what we talked about. I have someone for you to see on standby." He passed Harold a business card. "Take a three hour break. I'll inform Bandoff. Melonie will cancel all of your appointments."

Shannon's face twisted into a knot. Veins strained against her translucent skin. "I'll inform him too!" she barked.

Shannon despised Harold for leaving his wife. She lusted for him for years and he never even considered her for a mate. It bothered her to no end that Harold left his wife for an Arab. It irked her even more that her workplace seemed to resemble the United

Nations. Times like this she wished she had never left the conservative comforts of South Carolina.

"I'm sure you will," Melonie responded as she turned her petite frame on her heels and cut her eyes at Shannon.

"You're lucky you have a green card," Shannon sneered.

"You're lucky you're out of my reach," Melonie yelled back as she left the room.

Harold sat on his desk and wept like a small child. Tears ran down his pink skin as he blubbered silently. He picked up his phone and called the number on the card John gave him. A friendly psychiatrist answered and arranged an appointment with Harold.

Harold succumbed to defeat on the third afternoon.

Harold slept in the office until his phone rang.

"Yes Melonine."

"Miss Vahid is here to see you. She is looking cute too. Where are ya'll going?"

"Send her in." He hung up the phone.

Fatima walked into his office wearing an all black dress with black shoes and assurance.

"You look beautiful."

"Thanks. What happened to you?"

Harold's hair was wild and his shirt was wrinkled.

"I had a rough day."

"I see."

"Do you mind if we order and eat here?"

"No, I don't mind," Fatima replied. "I just wanted to see you."

"What do you want to eat?" asked Harold.

"Chicken."

"What kind?"

"It doesn't matter," she signed already bored by the idea of sitting in his office on such a beautiful day.

Harold pushed a button on the phone and asked Melonie to enter his office. The small woman walked in with her long black hair in a ponytail.

"You are looking good girl!" Fatima said to Melonie.

"You are the one!" she replied to Fatima.

"Are you two finished stroking each other's ego?" Harold snapped.

"No." They laughed in union.

"Well I'm hungry," he grumbled.

"Okay, Okay." Melonie said as she retrieved a pen from her pocket.

Harold and Fatima chose their food and Melonie went to call it in to the restaurant. About a half hour later the food arrived and the two ate lunch together. They finished their lunch, kissed, and said goodbye. Harold got back to work and worked well into the late evening.

Around eight o'clock John walked into Harold's office.

"Did you do it?" John asked while looking around at the mess that had been made. "Make the appointment?"

Harold looked up at his friend and mumbled, "Yeah."

"Good. I'm gone."

"Ciao."

"Peace out Man," John waved as he walked out of the office.

Harold straightened his desk, told Melonie to go home, and began to get ready to go himself. He gathered all of his belongings and picked up his car keys. Harold left the office building. Unfortunately, he was parked beside Shannon and she too was getting into her car.

"Have a good night." Harold said.

"I dare you! You pig!"

"Shannon, you are something else. Too bad you weren't something else in bed."

"Go to hell you low life. Genaline is better off dead than having to be humiliated by you!" Shannon roared. "I don't know which was worse, you leaving me for Genaline or you leaving Genaline for that sand nigger. I would kill myself too!"

Harold slammed his door and walked over to Shannon. He grabbed her by the neck and pressed her against the car.

"If you ever call her a nigger again I will snap your pretty neck in half. Do you understand me?"

"Yes!" she cried. Her face began to turn blue. Shannon could see the darkness coming.

"You are just angry because you don't have talent enough to satisfy a virgin and a plastic surgeon couldn't give a better shape to that body of yours!" He let her go and walked back to his car. "Ciao!"

Shannon fell back against her vehicle and watched him drive off. Her red hair was damp with sweat; her eyes overflowing with tears. She got into her vehicle; her frail skinny body trembling. Shannon placed her freckled hand upon her steering wheel. She closed the door and sat there for a while.

Harold turned on his radio and he listened to the soulful voice of Brandy singing in his car. His phone rang. He turned down the radio and picked up the phone.

"Hello."

"Shannon too! I was true to you. How many more were there?"

"Who is this?" Harold asked.

"I died for you?"

"Who the hell is this?" he yelled into the receiver.

"You forgot my voice already? Oh, I'm sorry. You barely remembered me in life. How can I expect for you to remember me in death?"

"Genaline?"

"I loved you!"

The phone hung up. Fear tortured Harold on the third evening.

Fatima heard the sound of Harold's car pulling into the driveway. She rushed to the door and opened it for him. Harold fell into her arms and wept.

"What's wrong?"

"Just hold me and never let go."

"Okay," Fatima agreed.

The couple stood in front of the door for at least a half hour. Harold broke the embrace and walked straight into the bedroom.

He threw all of his clothes on the floor and fell across the bed. Fatima walked in behind him.

"Are you hungry?" she asked.

"Yes."

She walked into the kitchen and pulled his plate out of the oven. Earlier she had prepared pork chops, broccoli and cheese, mashed potatoes, rolls, glazed carrots, and homemade lemonade. She put his food on a tray and brought it to him.

Harold sat up and ate everything quickly and quietly. He got up and went to the bar. He took a bottle of red wine and began to drink. Hours passed and he had guzzled down four bottles. He reached for the last corner of wine in the bottle and poured it into his glass. The liquid was thick and dark red. A voice whispered in his ear, "Drink. Be Merry. This is the blood I shed for you!" Harold jumped up and threw the glass across the room. Fatima ran in and stared at him.

"What's wrong!" Fatima screamed.

"Look at the wall!" Harold pointed.

"It is only wine! What?"

"It wasn't a minute ago. It was blood!" he slurred.

"You are insane Harold!"

"No I'm not. I'm telling you!"

"Look Harold!" Fatima yelled. "Go and touch it! You're acting stupid!"

Harold slowly stumbled over to the wall to examine the thin red liquid running down to the floor. It was wine on the wall. Harold secretly claimed insanity on the fourth night.

The alarm clock sounded and Harold got up for work. He ate cold cereal and headed out of the door. He didn't even bother to kiss Fatima good morning. He arrived at the office a half hour early and began on some paper work. He called and verified his one o'clock doctor's appointment and took a fifteen minute nap. Around nine, Melonie walked in and sat a hot cup of coffee on his desk. He gave her some paperwork and she went back to her desk. John and Mr. Bandoff walked into Harold's office.

"Hello gentlemen," Harold reluctantly greeted.

"Hello Harold." Bandoff replied.

"What up!" John said.

Bandoff looked at John and frowned.

"How are you Harold?" Bandoff asked.

"Fine and you Sir?"

"Never mind me. Did you and Miss Wheeler have a confrontation last night?"

"Yes Sir." Harold nodded slowly.

"She said you choked her. Is that true?" Bandoff asked. He clasped his hands behind his back and looked sternly into Harold's eyes.

"Yes I did Sir." Harold tried to keep a serious face. He wanted desperately to smirk. He so enjoyed wrapping his fingers around Shannon's throat.

"Good. She deserved it," Bandoff said smirking. "You better be thankful she didn't press charges. Don't let it happen again Bunden. Understand?"

"Yes Sir," Harold replied.

"Did you make an appointment?"

"Yes Sir."

"When?"

"Today at one."

"Very well. Get well. You are one of my best lawyers. I don't want to have to replace you with another partner. Understand?" Bandoff raised his eyebrow at Harold.

"Yes Sir."

"Ciao," Bandoff grumbled and turned to John. "Go to your office."

"Okay Sir," John replied.

Bandoff walked to the door and yelled over his shoulder, "Bunden, get back to work."

"Yes Sir," Harold replied.

Bandoff then walked out to the office. The old man's gray hair looked like a fizzy glow around his bald age spotted head. He walked out slowly revealing his age with every step.

Harold was intimidated on the forth morning.

Twelve thirty came around and Harold left his office to see Dr. Cummings. He arrived there at one o'clock on the dot and he was escorted into Dr. Cummings office by a very beautiful secretary. Harold tapped the woman's buttocks and walked into the office.

"Hello Obadele. It's been a long time. How is Latrice?" Harold asked.

"She is doing well. How are you and Genaline?"

"Genaline and I got separated," Harold answered.

"I'm sorry to hear that."

"She killed herself." Harold lowered his head and shook it slowly.

"My God!" Dr. Cummings exclaimed. "I'm so very sorry that happened to you and to her."

"Where do I sit Doc?"

"Wherever you please," answered Dr. Cummings as he stepped backwards to let Harold walk pass.

Harold sat on a long couch in front of Dr. Cummings.

"Harold, how can I help you?" Dr. Cummings asked.

"I have been seeing things. Hearing things. Genaline is haunting me."

"Haunting you?" Dr. Cummings raised his eyebrows. "Sometimes guilt can..." Dr. Cummings was quickly cut off.

"Yes, haunting me! She is angry because I left her. Genaline has even threatened to kill me."

"Really?" Dr. Cummings asked.

"Am I Crazy Doc?"

"Of course not." The tall ebony doctor stood and began to pace the floor. "Tell me more."

"Strange things have been happening. Genaline calls me on the phone. I've seen her in my bathroom. She left our wedding pictures in my dash board. I know I didn't put them there. I thought one of the secretaries at the firm was her."

"Does anyone see these things or hear these things besides you?"

"No." Harold paused. "Once Fatima saw blood on my robe. I didn't know where it came from. I just felt something wet on the wall, wiped my hand, and it was there. There was nothing wet there when I went back to look. How do you explain what's happening Doc?

"I don't know. Look at these pictures and tell me what you see," Dr. Obadele Cummings requested as he began to flip ink blots.

"I see a butterfly. I see a couple. A heart. Genaline!" Harold wailed. "I see Genaline lying in a pool of blood."

Dr. Cummings looked at the ink blot. All he saw was a flower with a dark petal in the middle. He shook his shoulders and looked at Harold.

"Harold, I think you are overly stressed. You obviously feel guilty and responsible. Tell me about her death."

"She jumped off our balcony. I wasn't with her. I was with Fatima."

"Fatima Vahid?"

"Yes. We were a couple." Harold cleared his throat. "I mean are a couple."

"Did Genaline know this?"

"Yes. She killed herself when I served her the divorce papers."

"Do you think that you are personally responsible for her death?" the doctor asked.

"I didn't know she would take it that hard!" Harold lowered his head and sobbed.

"Do you think that you are responsible?"

"Yes!"

"All of your hallucinations are from guilt. Free yourself of that guilt. It was not your fault that she died. Genaline made her own choice."

"But..."

"But nothing. You didn't tell her to take her life and you didn't take her life. I know it's difficult but you have to put your mind at rest. You are an innocent man."

"Yes Doc. I'll try. I will probably be more depressed after I get your bill." Harold forced a smile to his face.

"Well, I can't help you with that problem." Dr. Obadele Cummings smiled. He gave Harold his coat. "I have another patient waiting and you have already taken up ten minutes of her time. She needs it. She is a nut case," he laughed.

Harold took his coat and said goodbye. A small burden was lifted on the fourth afternoon.

Harold went back to his office and worked until seven p.m. He ran into Shannon again at the elevator. They both walked in.

"I'm sorry Harold."

"Forgiven."

"You knew how much I loved you. Do you even think about the way we use to be?" Shannon pushed the stop button on the elevator. She took off her coat and dropped her brief case and purse to the floor.

"What are you doing?" Harold asked; his eyes stretched wide.

"Just give me one more chance to make love to you. I know I could please you," Shannon begged.

Being the man that Harold was, he granted her wish. They made passionate love in the elevator. Shannon purposely kissed his collar and left a bit of perfume on his shirt.

After the deed was done, Harold got dressed and turned the elevator back on.

"How was it?" Shannon asked with a hopeful look in her eyes.

"The same way it always was. Nothing to write home about." He stepped out of the elevator and walked to his car.

Shannon screamed from the top of her lungs, "You self centered moron! I hate you!"

"I couldn't tell!" he yelled back.

Shannon ran from the elevator and cried all the way to her vehicle.

Harold got into his car and drove home. He was ignorant of the lipstick or the perfume on his shirt. He unlocked the door and walked in.

"Fatima!" Harold called.

"Yes."

"Come in here!"

"Okay," she replied as she ran into the living room. He picked her up and spun her around the room. She spied the lipstick.

"I feel great!" He confessed. "I went to see a doctor friend of mine today and…"

"What the hell is that!" She pointed at his collar.

"What?" Harold dismissed her and continued. "Not now honey. I saw Obadele today and I feel great."

"What is that lipstick doing on your shirt?" Fatima screamed. Anger flooded her eyes.

"What are you talking about?" He looked down. Lipstick was on his shirt.

"That!" She poked at the lipstick so hard that Harold could feel fer fingernail through his shirt.

"I don't know how that got there! I hugged an old lady client today." Harold lifted his shoulders with a dumb expression painted across his face.

Fatima looked closer and smelled the perfume. "Since when do old ladies where French perfume? You smell like a whore! I am no fool!" Fatima slapped him so hard that his neck popped. "Get out!"

"This is my home!" Harold roared. "You get out!"

"I can't believe you are sleeping around. I won't take this from you. I am not like that simple wife you had. I'll kill you!" Fatima huffed.

"Let me explain."

"Explain what? How you screwed her? How good it was? How sorry you are?" Fatima bellowed.

"I didn't do anything!" Harold lied. "You don't trust me?"

"Damn right I don't!"

"I hugged Mr. Bandoff's wife. She kissed me. Call and ask!" He picked up the phone. "Call!"

"I don't want to call!"

"Call the woman! You accused me! Call!"

"I'm sorry."

"Forgiven."

Harold concealed a lie on the fourth night.

Harold woke up in a great mood. He and Fatima made love all night and his mind was far from Genaline. He showered, dressed and left for work. He skipped breakfast and ran to his car. He arrived at work on time for his 8:45 meeting with a smile on his face.

"Looking good!" John complimented.

"I agree." Bandoff said with his shaky voice. "Don't you agree Shannon?"

"No." She sneered. "Not at all."

The remaining people showed up for the meeting. Cases were discussed and decisions were made. Bandoff stood up and straightened his tie.

"Attention everyone! I have a new person to introduce to the firm."

A dark haired white woman stepped through the door.

Harold screamed.

Everyone turned to him.

"G...G...Genaline!" He trembled.

The woman looked surprised.

"My name is Dorthy Baker." She put out her hand.

Harold ran out of the room.

"I guess he didn't like me," Dorthy Baker joked. She smiled and took a seat.

Shannon laughed aloud. John went to find Harold. Bandoff was furious. Humiliation reigned on the fifth morning.

Harold slept in his car until about noon. He then entered his office and began some paper work. His phone rang.

"Melonie, what?"

"Bandoff is here to..."

The door flew open.

"I am sick of you Bunden! You obviously have a problem. I am sending you on a two week vacation and if you are not well by then you are fired!" Bandoff slammed the door and left Harold's office.

Harold gathered his things and left the office. He went to John's office and knocked on the door.

"Come in," John said.

Harold walked in.

"Get well man. You got two weeks. I don't want to lose you."

"I will," Harold said, "Thanks for looking out for me."

"Harold, you really shouldn't have slept with Shannon again. She has told half of the secretaries in the building."

"No wonder Melonie is mad at me," Harold exclaimed.

"Don't let Fatima find out," John advised.

"I won't."

"Peace man."

"Ciao."

Harold got into his car and drove around the city for a few hours. He arrived at home around two and thoughts of losing his job permeated his mind on the fifth afternoon.

Fatima came home with Melonie with her around eight that night. The two women walked right past Harold and went into the bedroom. Harold picked up the remote and hit the mute button. He took his foot off the table and looked toward the bedroom.

"You two could speak!" he yelled.

No one answered.

"Why are you home so late?" Harold asked.

No one answered. He got up and walked into the bedroom. Fatima was packing and Melonie was helping her.

"What are you doing?" Harold asked Fatima.

"You liar! Why Shannon? That vengeful twit. You are so stupid," Fatima wailed.

"No Fatima! Don't go!" He grabbed her arm. She hit him. He let go. She slapped him and began to punch him wildly. Melonie tried to pull her back. Fatima knocked her down.

"I hate you!" Fatima spit in his face. She resumed packing and she and Melonie walked out of the house.

"Muy es feo punta," Melonie yelled at Harold. She slammed the door in his face.

Fatima left Harold on the fifth night.

Morning came and Harold didn't sleep a wink. He sat on his bed and stared at pictures of Fatima and pictures of Genaline. Tears ran down his cheek as he sat in complete silence. He had nowhere else to go. He had nothing at home to want to stay. Days passed and he ate butter toast and cold cereal. He watched trendy talk shows and bored himself with soap operas. He didn't brush his teeth or shower. His beard grew in and his blonde hair was tangled all over his head like one dreadlock. Depression grabbed a hold of him on the sixth morning.

Time passed on. The days got longer. He fixed himself a ham and cheese sandwich and some chips. He visited his bar every thirty minutes. Around two thirty the phone rang.

"Fatima?"

"No. It's John. How are you?"

"I'm bad man. I'm really bad. Fatima left me."

"I heard. Shannon has been in a great mood all day. I told you that was bad news."

"Yeah! Yeah! Life sucks."

"Take care. I got an appointment coming in. See you soon. Get well. Peace Man!"

"Ciao." Harold hung up. He walked to the couch and sat down.

The door bell rang.

"Who is it?"

"Special delivery," a voice from outside answered.

He opened the door a man handed him a note. The note read:

Harold,
I'm glad you are suffering. I suffered because of you. I left you a gift. Go to the hall closet and open the gift box.
Genaline

Harold went to the closet and swung open the door. His eyes quickly found a beautifully wrapped gift box. He grabbed the box. He opened it and immediately dropped the box to the floor. He backed away from the bloody human heart that had fallen from the box. Harold grabbed his phone and called the police. When the cops arrived, he showed them a blank piece of paper (the note) and a box with a paper valentine inside.

"Real funny Sir," the cop said.

"I tell you it was a real heart," Harold insisted.

"Sure and I'm Santa Claus and he is the Tooth Fairy," one cop responded sarcastically. "It's against the law to prank call the police."

Harold apologized and asked the cops to leave. He plopped down in his living room and wept. Frustration ruled him on the seventh evening.

Harold paced the house nonstop for hours and hours. He jumped at every sound. He jumped every time the phone rang and trembled every time he thought he heard a knock on the door. He sat in a corner and wept until his eyes ached and his throat dried.

Suddenly, he looked up. He heard a voice calling him. He stood up. The voice told him to go home. Go to his real home. He picked up his keys and drove across town to the penthouse that he had shared with Genaline. He took the door key from under a flower pot and opened the door. Inside was the sweet smell of roses. They were Genaline's favorite. He walked through the house looking at all the pictures they had taken together. They were everywhere. They were so happy. He smiled. He saw a shadow on the balcony. He walked out there and he saw Genaline standing on the balcony. She looked so beautiful. Her black hair looked so glossy and her body looked gorgeous in her thin night gown.

"Genaline," he called out. "I'm sorry."

"Forgiven," she cooed.

"Can I hold you?" he begged.

"Yes. Come to me," Genaline beckoned with arms wide open.

He stepped up on the balcony.

"Come to me," she summoned him with eyes full of sadness and love.

Harold reached out for her and she disappeared. He lost his balance and fell off of the balcony. Moments later, he was lying on the ground lifeless. A crowd formed around his body trying hard not to step on the scarlet mess he had made. The moon and the stars shined on the seventh night and Harold rested.

DO YOU LOVE ME?

"Loneliness. That's my worst fear. To walk through eternity alone, un-loved, empty." She looked into the eyes of her lover and turned away from him with her head hanging low. She ran her hand over her short kinky hair. Her beautiful face showed no trace of emotion. Latrice sat upon the bed staring at a life sized painting of her and her lover on the wall. The black and white portrait was framed in thin gold and the couple was nude with only a cloth hiding the sacred parts of their bodies. In the picture, they were engaged in a deep embrace.

"I love you Latrice. Why do you feel so all alone?" the tall ebony man asked with concern. His slender form was sprawled across the bed like a load of sorted laundry. "I'm always here for you." He put his hand on her shoulder, softly pushing the strap of her purple tank-top to the side. Her back was turned to him as she sat on the edge of the bed.

"I love you too Austin. But you will not always be here. Don't make promises that you can't keep." She turned to him and smiled a pitiful smile.

Austin was flushed with anger. It seemed to him that he would never be able to convey his love for her.

"I hate it when you say things like that! How do you know if I will be around or not? If you end up being alone, it will be because you shut me and everyone else who loves you out of your life!"

"Austin," she whispered. Latrice grabbed his chin softly and tried to pull his face close to hers.

"No! Listen to me!" He pushed her hand away. "We've been dating for eight months and I don't know much about you! I don't know where you live, work, or where you go when you leave here in the wee-hours of the morning."

"Austin!" she lifted her sweet voice.

He sat up beside her. His forehead wrinkled and a small vein appeared on his temple.

"No! Let me finish! You're lonely because you choose to be. I want to be with you forever but I'm a fool to want such a thing. You refuse to tell me your age, where you were born, anything about your family, or any other normal thing a person is suppose to share with someone they love! You don't trust me!"

"Austin." She put her hand on his trembling knee. "You don't understand. I am not like others. You wouldn't understand my lifestyle. You would probably want nothing to do with me if you knew how I lived."

"You make it sound like you're a serial killer or something. Tell me." Austin paused and squinted his eyes and stared deep into hers. Pique and suspicion clouded his face. "Are you a hooker?"

"Of course not." She rolled her eyes, insulted by the lewd accusation.

"A drug addict or dealer?" Austin huffed.

"Don't be silly!"

"A murderer?" he asked.

"Not unless provoked. Besides, isn't that the same thing as a serial killer?" She smacked her lips, crossed her arms, and sighed.

"What? Are you saying that you kill when you feel like you're provoked?"

"Self-defense you irrational angel!" She let a smile decorate her strong but beautiful facial features. "I'm not a menace to society dear. I'm just not a part of society."

"Do you care to explain?" Austin asked.

"No," she declined.

"You see!" He jumped up and stared in the mirror. Behind him Latrice went to the other side of the room quicker than a flash of lightning. Austin spun around astonished by her speed. He was almost speechless. "What...what? How did you do that?"

"Do what?" she asked with a small tremble in her voice.

"Cross the room so quickly."

"I just got up and moved," Latrice mumbled.

"Why?"

She crossed her arms and replied, "I just wanted too."

"Why do you fear looking at yourself? Are you afraid of what you may see? You refuse to look in the mirror or take pictures. What's the problem? You're the most beautiful woman that I have ever seen. I can't image you or anyone thinking differently."

"I just don't like pictures," Latrice said. She hated when he interrogated her.

"Are you that insecure about yourself that you damn your own reflection?" yelled Austin as his eyes burned deep into hers.

Latrice was getting ruffled.

"It has little to do with insecurity!" she spat, avoiding eye contact. Never could she look at him when she was angry.

"Why then?"

"Why what Austin? Why what? We weren't even on this subject!" Latrice opened a drawer and picked out a fresh pair of underwear and took a towel from the closet shelf. She also picked up a small pouch filled with soft soil.

.   "What are you doing?" Austin yelled.

Latrice took a deep breath. Her shoulders began to tense up. She answered him between her teeth, "Going to take a shower. Is there a problem with that?"

"Yes it is! Every time you go to take a shower you sprinkle dirt on the floor of the bathroom. Why take a shower if you want to stay dirty?"

Latrice avoided his eyes. She was furious.

"I have to go soon. I need to go pick up something to eat!" she said.

"That's another thing! Why won't you even go to dinner with me?"

"I don't like the type of food you like," she barked.

"I'm positive that someone in this city can prepare a dish that we both will find delectable." Sarcasm rolled from his tongue as he crossed his arms and stared at her.

"I don't think so." She walked towards the bathroom. Austin grabbed her arm with a firm grip. She shook him loose easily.

A look of surprise crossed his face. Sometimes he was simply amazed by her strength. He scratched his head full of curly hair and sighed.

"Wait a minute okay! I want to talk and you will not walk away!"

"Don't tell me what I will not do!" she yelled as she stared at the floor.

"Look at me Latrice. You always avoid my eyes when you're angry. Let me see how you feel. Show me that I mean something. I need to see some emotion."

"No." Latrice said simply.

"You're shutting me out!" he screamed as he grabbed the sides of his head in desperation. "Talk to me!"

"You don't understand. You don't know what it means to love someone like me!" A red tear formed in her eye.

"Don't cry baby!" He paused. "Are you okay? You okay? Your eye is ...bleeding."

She wiped the crimson tear away quickly.

"I am fine," she whined. "May I go to the shower now?"

"No Latrice. Tonight we settle this once and for all. I will not live like this any longer. I want to know if you really love me?"

"Yes, Austin, but it's so much pain. So much." She lifted her eyes to meet his. The anger was gone.

He touched her cheek delicately.

"Tell me something, what is it that you are hiding?" Austin asked.

"I can't. You won't understand."

"I love you. I would die for you girl. Can't you see that?"

Latrice's face wrinkled. She grabbed her side and grimaced in pain.

"Austin I need to drink. I have to leave," she whimpered.

"No!" Austin exclaimed. He pulled her close to him to support her crippling body. "What's wrong? Maybe I can fix you something."

"No! I need to leave!" Latrice pulled herself away from Austin but he would not let her go.

"Please let me help you. What can I do? If you're sick, let me give you something. If you're hurt, let me take you to the doctor," Austin pleaded.

"I said no!" Latrice screamed into his face, her breath as icy as the North Pole.

Tell me what to do!" Austin demanded. "I give you my love. I promise you forever. What do you want from me?"

She looked into his dark brown eyes. Fright grabbed onto his soul as he stared into her blood red eyes. The whites of her eyes looked like dark pools of scarlet; her irises fire yellow.

"What are you?" He backed away.

"I am what you would never understand."

He walked toward her slowly. He could not bear seeing her in pain. She looked frightful but the sight of her pain twisted body was more frightening. His love was greater than his fear. He reached out to her.

"No! Come no closer!" Latrice screamed; her voice a snarling roar.

"I love you Latrice!" He walked on.

She stood upright; a puzzling look in her eyes. Her head moved to the side like a curious puppy. Red tears rolled down her golden freckled cheeks.

"I love you Latrice. Come to me and let me help you."

She walked to him and placed her hand upon his shoulder.

"Do you love me?" she asked; her eyes glowing intensely.

"Yes, I love you." Austin walked slowly into her open arms.

She kissed his eyelids, his nose, his cheek. She showered his cinnamon brown shoulders with kisses.

"Do you love me?" she asked again as she tongued his ear and licked down his salty sweet neck.

"Yes, I love you." He cooed with pleasure.

"Do you really love me?" She ran her fingers down the small of his back and kissed his light chocolate collarbone.

"Yes." He wrapped his strong arms around her tiny waist. His hands glided across her voluptuous hips. He kissed the smooth of her chest. "Yes, I love you."

"Will you give your life for me?" Latrice asked in a whisper sending airy butterflies into his ears.

"Yes." He caressed her breasts with his strong hands. "Yes."

Latrice looked into his eyes and began to kiss his neck. "Promise?"

"I promise," he whispered as he allowed his neck to fall beneath her rain of kisses.

Latrice held her head back as four large fangs broke through her gums and protruded from her mouth. Two fangs came from the top center of her mouth and two came from the bottom center. Latrice installed the razor sharp fangs as her long abnormal tongue lapped at the escaping blood. She drank for a short while and released her lover. Latrice stared at the wounds and command them to be healed. They disappeared without a trace. A strange power flowed through her body. The feeling made her head swim.

"Austin!" she called out. She kissed his ear trying to dismiss the sensation. Her head swooned with intoxicated bliss.

"Yes," he answered, unblinking.

"I will not make you as I am." She ran her fingers through his short curls. He was so beautiful to her. His face always reminded her of someone she knew long long ago. A face lost within the corridors of her mind. She could never quite put her finger on it. That reminder was the very thing that drew her to Austin in the first place.

"I know." He pulled her closer.

"I love you too much," she said.

"I love you too. Much more than you know." A peculiar smile bent his lips.

"Why are not afraid of me?" asked Latrice, puzzled by his acceptance and lack of fear.

"I was the one who created you Latrice, formally Salima of Morocco, one hundred and fifty-nine years ago. I was hypnotized by your beauty and I watched you sleep every night until one night I could no longer restrain my urge to have you. I fed from you while you slept. I knew the moment I saw your face that I had to spend eternity with you. You left Africa long ago and I spent years searching for you. Now that I have you back with me, never will we part."

"What are you talking about?" Latrice broke his embrace and stepped backwards. Confusion and shock filled her eyes. *My feeding must have made him delirious.*

Austin smiled as his eyes turned completely black and six razor sharp fangs came from his mouth.

"I love you. Now, do you still love me?"

THE ROAD NOT TAKEN

"Bring, bring, bring!" the alarm clock sounded over and over again trying to awaken Clarissa. Like always, she reached over with a natural reflex and hit the snooze button. Time crept by slowly but surely.

"Bring, bring, bring!" the alarm clock rang for the very last time. Clarissa wiped away the last of the sandman's dust from her eyes and pulled herself into a sitting position.

"What time is it?" she asked herself as she fumbled for the lamp switch. "Oh goodness! I am running late," she screamed as she ran hurriedly to the shower. She undressed with the swiftness of Conan's sword and leapt into the steamy shower. The hot water drenched every inch of her as bubbles covered her body as she scrubbed quickly. Clarissa rinsed and stepped onto the cold floor dripping. Wet footsteps lay stagnant throughout the hall as she ran into her bedroom and picked up the telephone. Her fingers danced across the numbered cubes as she fumbled with her towel, trying to dry herself.

"Hello," Kyre said through the receiver.

"Hi. Sorry I am running late. I will be on the way in a sec. I kinda over slept. We can still make it before it gets too late. I heard that this is gonna be the biggest night in the history of our town. This club is supposed to be the hottest club in the south. Tell Kery to get dressed," said Clarissa while rambling through her drawers trying to find a fresh pair of underwear.

"Okay," said Kyre. "We'll be ready soon. See ya!"

Clarissa hung up the phone and got dressed, ate a banana, and ran to the car realizing that she had left the keys in the door. She ran back and snatched the delaying object out of the door and hit the road. Fifteen minutes passed and she arrived at the humble home of Kyre and Kery. Kyre, a very pretty, short, light skinned girl came running out of the door while her tall brown skinned, curly haired brother Kery lagged behind.

"Come on!" yelled Clarissa. "We gotta go!"

"Oh shut up! You are the one who's late. Don't try to rush now," said Kery as he slowed his pace, trying hard to irritate his sister and her best friend.

"Boy, if you don't get your butt in this car all you will see are my tail lights," Clarissa snapped.

The car flew down the street, up a rarely traveled side road, across a dark dirt road, and past a large meadow. They arrived at their destination in about twenty minutes. A sane driver would have gotten there in thirty. They pulled into the parking lot of a very secluded location, pausing to look at the beautiful yet frightening site before them.

A banner that read, "Grand Opening," draped the front of the gigantic building. So peculiar looking was the structure, it made their bellies bubble with excitement. The building was painted black with sparkling silver spider webs on the walls. A set of electronic swirling eyes sat above a sign which read, "The Road Not Taken."

"Well, we're here," said Clarissa as she pulled a tube of lip gloss from her purse to retouch her lips.

"It looks cool," Kery said while fingering his barbiche, a small tuff of curls caressing his bottom lip.

"I don't know. It's a little on the strange side. Don't you think? What kind of crowd is this anyway?" asked Kyre.

"I don't know but we'll soon find out," Clarissa answered, her emerald eyes not leaving the façade of the club.

Clarissa parked the car and the three went inside.

The club was a separate brick building inside of the outside frame. Between the building and the frame was a long line consisting of all types of people waiting to get inside of the club. There were hip hop dressers, surfer kids, sleek and stylish people, slutty ladies, biker boys, rough necks, and conservatives. The variety was simply amazing.

The inside of the club was even more bizarre than the outside. Pitch black walls with red lights in the shape of eyes covered the walls and ceilings. Purple plastic gargoyles stood at the entrances and exits. The music had a mysterious rhythm that made the hair on the back of the neck stand up as it provoked the body to move to its tempting beat. The bar, the tables, and the chairs were all painted in a deep glowing scarlet. Most alarming was the dance floor. It was mammoth. The entire floor was made of glass. Under the floor, heatless fire burned. Steam burst from all corners of the dance floor and gave off a reddish gold foggy glow. All in all, it was a phenomenal sight.

"This is too much. It looks like some old psycho stuff. I don't know about this place. It gives me chills," said Kyre as chills crawled up her neck like a million leg bug.

"I think it's hot!" said Clarissa. "I can dig this place. It's really different. Creative. Yeah. That's what it is. Creative."

"Too freaking creative," snapped Kery sarcastically. "This looks like some satanic crap. I don't need to be here," Kery concluded as he started to walk towards the door. Clarissa grabbed his arm. He gave her the evil eye and she turned him loose.

"Oh come on. Let's stay. We paid fifteen dollars and I want to party," Clarissa begged.

"For a little while," Kery said in an uneasy tone.

Clarissa walked across the club. Her body danced against the red lights. Her short brown hair shined with auburn hues as her small waist and ample hips faded into the steam of the dance floor.

"That girl is fine," Kery mumbled to himself.

"Boy, get your eyes off my friend. She should be like a sister to you by now," Kyre said, punching him in the arm.

"Whatever! I aint got but one sister and she aint her!"

Kyre laughed and walked off into the red glow of the club. Kery stood in place for a moment then decided to make his way to the bar. He paused when he reached the counter and let his eyes rest upon an odd looking barmaid. She was ghostly white; the kind of white that porcelain dolls possessed. It wasn't normal. Her eyes were a clear yellow and they were lined with black make-up smeared badly. Jet black hair with red streaks through it stood wild all over her head. Every wrinkle on her lips was dark as if they cracked and bled and dried. Thick gloss covered their crackly flesh.

"May I help you?" the barmaid asked.

Kery's eyes rested upon her nametag. It read, "Spider."

"Yeah, let me get some gin and juice. More gin than juice," he ordered.

"Coming right up."

"So Spider, who thought of this club? It's a unique idea," Kery asked, eyeing his surroundings as he inhaled the disturbing details: a growling clock on the wall, a fountain pouring a thick substance resembling blood, a man in a corner with his eyes rolled backwards and a needle dangling from his arm, and two women sandwiching a boy who was way too young to be in the club.

"Yes, unique it is. It is another world." Spider flashed an evil smile.

"You got that right." Kery took a sip. "Outta space."

"No. Out of reality," she winked.

Kery looked at her with a side glance of disapproval. He picked up his drink and moved away from the bar.

"Time for me to pick up some ladies," he whispered.

Like a beckoning nymph, the dance floor drew everyone in the club to it. The music growled through the speakers and the people began to grind, roll, and become hypnotized by the rhythm of the music. Sensual moves changed into violent slam dancing. Unnatural aggression took over the men. Erotic longing engulfed the women. The entire club rocked in a demonic rhythm that eliminated every individual's sense of self.

Kyre found herself messaging her body in the most titillating fashion. When flashes of reality hit her, she would attempt to break from the crazed trance but the music would roar and try to bring her back under its spell. It succeeded and she migrated back to the dance floor.

Suddenly, the dance floor trembled, rumbled, shook with dizzying force. Everyone ran to the edge of the floor. As soon as the floor was cleared, it divided. A small platform rose from the center of the floor. On the platform stood a horrible looking couple clinging to one another in an outlandish manner. The woman's arm draped around the man's neck as her free hand flicked his elongated nipple. Her legs wrapped tightly around his back. Their skin was pale and bluish. Dark hair swirled all over their heads like spider webs. They looked so similar that they could have been related. Black cloth hung from their nude bodies.

The woman yelled, "Welcome to 'The Road Not Taken.' We are glad you have taken it!" she cackled. "Big Daddy is pleased with you all. Thank you for coming to see us."

The man called Big Daddy nodded. He flashed a smile showing fanged teeth. The crowd gasped.

"Don't mind us," the woman yelled. "Go on. Dance." The couple laughed a bone chilling laugh in unison.

The dance floor closed around the platform and the people reluctantly poured back onto the floor, oblivious to the couple in the center. The couple on the platform began to grind their bodies together as if they were devouring one another. The music came to a halt. Time stood still. Silence reigned. The couple danced on, their bodies fusing, melting into one flesh; into one being; a supernatural thing; an astonishing creature; a beast.

The emerald green beast stood about nine feet tall. It had the body of a muscular male but the face of a woman. Five inch claws protruded from its hands and feet like great eagle talons. The mighty jaw of the creature was heavily decorated with ivory spikes and narrow sharp teeth. Its eyes slanted with destruction.

The music resumed and the people danced. Kery stopped in mid motion. The daze wore off and he spied the creature in the middle of the dance floor flailing its arms as if it was directing a morbid symphony.

Kery pushed his way through the crowd and found Kyre and Clarissa.

"Let's go!" he yelled, pulling the girls toward him so hard that they both almost hit the floor.

Kyre snapped out of the spell quickly but Clarissa, with eyes glazed over, kept dancing. The siblings shook Clarissa violently until it seemed as if her bones were about to break. Clarissa fell to the floor and bumped her head.

"Are you okay?" Kyre asked as she bent down to hold her friend's head. "Say something!"

Clarissa opened her eyes. The fog over her pupils was gone.

"Let's go!" Kery yelled as he pulled Clarissa up and grabbed his sister's hand. He pushed through the crowd and forcefully pulled them behind him.

The trio headed towards the door. The purple gargoyles opened their eyes and stretched their arms wide to block the doorway. Clarissa screamed. Kery grabbed her mouth and began to run towards another exit. Kyre quickly followed. When they came to exit after exit, the same thing happened.

"What are we gonna do!" Kyre cried.

"Stay calm," Kery spat.

"How can we stay calm?" Clarissa bawled. "We can't get out of here!"

"We will find a way. We just have to stick together." Kery said as he searched the room with his eyes, looking for a way out.

Kery picked up a bar stool and held it high over his head with full intention of breaking the blocking arms of the gargoyles.

The music stopped. The head of the beast turned in slow motion ticks like the second hand on a clock. It looked down at them and a bellowing voice rumbled from its mouth.

"Dance my children. Dance for me. Don't leave. Daddy doesn't want you to leave. Be good for daddy," its voice echoed like thunder.

Kery smashed the chair against the arms of the gargoyles but the chair shattered into trillions of pieces. He ducked under the arms of the gargoyles but they lowered themselves. Kery attempted to leap over the arms but they became higher.

"Dance my children," the beast thundered. "Do not anger me. Dance now!" the beast stumped its gigantic foot. It shook its big head and let out a quiet growl. Saliva dripped from its maw as it narrowed its eyes. "Be good for daddy!"

Kyre screamed, "Let us out of here! You are not my daddy, my father, my anything. Let us go!" her fist balled tight and perspiration and sweat dripped from her quivering cheeks.

"Who is your father? Is he your father which art in heaven? I am he. Come worship me. Dance for me. This is heaven!" the beast growled. It clapped its hands together and the room quaked.

"You are not our father! This isn't heaven! Please release us from this hell!" Clarissa begged. She dropped to her knees and wept silently, her hair falling over her face casting her sobs in shadow.

The beast's eyes sparked. It let out an ear piercing growl.

"What!" the beast exploded. "You belittle my divinity? I am not thy father?" the beast huffed. It leaned forward and steam rose from its nostrils. "You detestable excuse for humanity! I am the god of the earth and all that dwells in it! Are you not thankful for this paradise that I have created for you? It was your desire when you received the flyer that promised you a night of seductive music and total debauchery. You could not wait to get here when you imagined taking a stranger home to bed or grinding your bodies against strange flesh and drinking yourselves unconscious!" the beast beat its chest. "I am thy father! Are you too superior to worship me?" the beast stepped from the platform. It licked its claws with a huge serpentine tongue. "I punish disobedience. The father loves whom he chastises. Why can't you be good for daddy?"

The trio tried to break through the exit again to no avail. All of the clubbers stood as if dead. Their swaying bodies showed no signs of life. Silence filled the air. Only the clicking claws of the demon's feet hitting the floor echoed through the room. Its slow steps towards the trio made chills run down their spines.

A great flame engulfed the head of the beast like hair. Its female face smiled. It spoke. "Be good for daddy. Daddy doesn't want to harm you." The beast spread its arms wide in an inviting gesture as it closed in on them. "Come give daddy a kiss. All I want is to give you pleasure."

The trio screamed in unison and ran for dear life. The annoyed demon sped up; its claws sounding like tap dancing shoes.

"Blasphemers! Come and worship me! Be good to daddy. Honor me!"

The demon rushed towards them. The trio split up. Each of them tried to hide themselves but everything they ducked behind vanished. There was no way out. The demon had them. The three ran to one another once again and joined quaking hands with tears running down each of their cheeks and fear bending their mouths in bows.

"Oh Jesus help us!" Kyre screamed.

The beast stopped in its tracks. Its diabolical eyes zoomed in on her and it yelled, "Never speak that name before me you fool! He has taken many of my children away in the name of his father who is unparallel to me! I am your daddy! Come to me! Do not betray me. I have given you worldly delights. Come to daddy!"

"Lord, help us!" wailed Kery. "Forgive us and help us God!"

"Stop it!" the beast yelled. Its foot melted into the floor. It tried to pull its leg free from the liquid but its flesh became as candle wax beneath flame.

"Father God in the name of Jesus, have mercy!" Kyre cried.

"Damn you!" the beast screamed as its body began to peel like the skin of a banana. It's flesh dropping to the ground like flakes.

"God help us!" Clarissa cried.

The beast cackled. "You have no faith! You are my child!" it yelled as its skin began to regenerate. Raw sores became smooth and its liquefied foot connected to its leg in reverse and solidified.

Clarissa stepped backwards. Her eyes stretched and her lips trembled. Panic claimed her body as she witnessed the beast become whole again.

"Have mercy upon our souls God!" Kyre submitted her supplication.

The beast let out an agonizing wail. Its arms began to bleed from each pore like scarlet polka dots joining into dripping lines.

"Free us, Lord, from the grasp of this demon. In the name of Jesus, God help us. Please give your angels charge over us. Protect us with your holy spirit," Kery wept.

The beast cried out. An enormous gash spilt his stomach. Its insides spilled out onto the floor. It clutched its pouring belly and fell hard against the floor.

"What have you done to me!" it screeched.

The twins prayed and praised the name of God and begged for salvation.

"Silence you infidels!" the beast squealed as its body began to turn to dust limb by limb. "Silence..." its voice echoed through the room as it became no more.

The gargoyles became lifeless again and moved back to their original positions. The spell was lifted from the people. Confusion and the smell of burning flesh permeated their noses. The dance floor split and tongues of fire leapt up from beneath and consumed many. A human stampede rushed the exits. The three narrowly escaped the building before the entire structure collapsed into a heap of dust and smoke.

The trio made it to the car. Kery opened the door for the ladies and they all dove inside. Kery took the wheel and sped from the parking lot; the tires screaming and leaving black skid marks on the concrete. In the rearview mirror, Kery saw a bright moonbeam surround the place where the club stood and faint winged silhouettes ascending to the heavens. He blinked and the beam was gone. He exhaled.

Clarissa wiped the tears from her eyes and turned on the radio. She leaned back. Loud heavy metal rang through the speakers when suddenly a deep agonizing voice vibrated through the car, "Daddy will be back! Be good for daddy!"

Kery punched the radio so hard that sparks flew through the car. He pushed the gas to the floor and the three sped into the dark of night; fading into the moonlight; disappearing into black.

THE MAKING OF AN ANGEL

Within quiet hills spread dark and wide, a miracle transpired during a lost moment in time. Long ago when the world was young and the heart of mankind was still partially pure, an evil hibernated deep within a mysterious land waiting for a chance to become.

"Come to me my darling," a small woman summoned with a wave of her hand and a bright twinkle in her eye. She sat upon a dark high back chair with wooden arms and legs. Its cushions were the deepest shade of violet and made of the plushest velvet.

"Come to me," she spoke again quietly. Her skin was golden and wrinkled. She looked as if she was once beautiful. Two slits were her eyes. Her nose was small and flat. Her face was round and her hair midnight black and pulled back into a short spiky ponytail. She wore a pale pink silk caftan decorated with small fuchsia dragons. Wrapping her arms around her daughter, she spoke in a soft secretive voice. "Ashley, I am getting old and my days with you are growing shorter by the moment."

"Please don't speak that way mother." Ashley hugged her mother close. "Don't speak of leaving me." Her mouth turned downward and she nestled her chin softly into her mother's shoulder blade.

"You are a woman now Ashley and I need to show you many things before it is too late. I feel a nefarious force within our homeland and it is up to you to destroy it. For many nights I have been plagued by dreams. You are a messiah, a savior of the people. I must prepare you for the great future for which you are destined." The woman let her arms fall free of her daughter and sat back in the chair. Bright yellow light danced across her face; a reflection from the fire she sat in front of. Her daughter, a younger twin of herself, sat on the floor in front of her cross-legged and wearing an ensemble similar to her mother's but in beige.

"I am no savior," Ashley exclaimed. "How can I destroy anything? I am powerless. I am ignorant of the creature's nature and power."

"So you feel its presence too my child?"

"Yes mother. I dream of it bellowing in the sea calling to anyone who will dare to face it. This beast is a manifestation of virginal evil and its power could virtually be unstoppable. I cannot see its form. Its existence is vague but there. It beckons me to challenge it." Ashley bowed her head and let her raven hair fall into her face in a perfect angle. A deep sigh left her lips.

"I was right," her mother said, caressing her child's shoulder and lifting her chin. A narrow line of tears ran down Ashley's cheek. Her mother wiped the tears away with one clean stroke.

"Do not worry. When the time comes, you will be mighty. Power from within will flow from you and you will cast the beast into oblivion."

"How?" The girl sighed.

"Come with me." Ashley's mother extended her hand and Ashley took it.

On the wall directly behind the chair was a life-sized painting of Tiashi the Mystic, Ashley's mother, when she was eighteen; Ashley's age now. Tiashi the Mystic whispered a chant and the painting became pellucid. The two women exited the dark chamber through the painting on the wall which led to a narrow hallway lit by red fiery torches. At the very end of the hall was a thick iron door fastened with rusted locks from top to bottom. A large iron beam rested securely across the middle of the door.

"Open, I command you," Tiashi the Mystic let the words roll of off her tongue with ease.

The locks unfastened one by one. The beam rose up and the door screeched open slowly. A gust of wind blew dust into Ashley's face. Tears instantly formed in her reddening eyes and she winced. The girl wiped the gray mess from her face and followed her mother into the dark room.

"Let there be light," Tiashi the Mystic commanded. And there was light.

The room was circular with scarlet walls. Pale red, almost pink, was the color of the ceiling and floor. One half of the room was filled with old books and scrolls. The books were in towering stacks covered with dust and withering from old age. Scrolls littered the floor on each side of the books. The handles of the scrolls were decorated with the finest metals and stones; artifacts taken from many ancient lands.

In the other half of the room, there was a round table made of teak wood surrounded by six round stools. Three fat candles sat in the center of the table with giant flames blazing unnaturally bright casting the room in pure white light. A round ivory tub with strange markings carved into it sat next to the table filled to the brim with thick crimson liquid. It bubbled quietly as little puffs of crimson steam burst from it and floated into the stale air forming fluffy red clouds.

"What is this place?" Ashley searched her mother's eyes for an explanation.

"The purification chamber." The older woman walked over to the highest stack of books and pulled a large one from the center of the stack. The other books fell into place undisturbed. "Please sit." Tiashi the Mystic pointed toward the table.

Ashley did as she was told and sat upon one of the dusty teak wood stools. She folded her slender golden fingers around one another and laid her hands upon her lap.

Tiashi the Mystic laid the big book upon the table and opened it. She lifted her hands into the air and chanted in an ancient tongue.

A sharp chill followed by a white hot burning sensation rocked Ashley's being. A dull red glow covered her body and she began to levitate. Red lightning shot from the walls and struck Ashley's floating body. The room quaked. The table and chairs, books and scrolls leapt off of the floor like frogs on hot coals. Tiashi the Mystic stood firm and chanted louder and louder until her voice became roaring thunder.

Ashley suffered a seizure in mid-air. Her eyes rolled back into her head and every hair on her head stood erect. Yellow foam dripped from her mouth and ran from her nose. Her convulsing body floated above the bubbling tub and the glow faded away.

Tiashi the Mystic fainted into silence and Ashley dropped into the warm tub of liquid. The script on the side of the tub pulsated with vibrant pink light. Red goo covered Ashley like thick strawberry syrup. Ashley pulled herself into a sitting position. Her eyes were spread wide and her mind dazed.

Tiashi the Mystic, slowly regained consciousness and the lightning stopped. She walked over to her daughter and pulled her out of the tub. She wiped the thick liquid from her child's face.

"Ashley!" She shook her.

Ashley opened her eyes. She stood motionless and dumbfounded.

"Ashley!" Tiashi the Mystic slapped her lightly. "Come back to me!" She shook her daughter frantically. "Come back!" Tears formed heavy puddles in the corners of her eyes. "Please come back!"

Ashley began to cough hysterically. Red goo poured from her gaping mouth. Her mother stepped backwards and a red glow covered Ashley once more. The goo evaporated and the glow vanished. Ashley stood before her mother clean and perfectly groomed. Every hair was in place and her skin was as clean and clear as freshly fallen rain. She held her head high and wisdom shined within her eyes.

"It is time." Tiashi the Mystic held her daughter close. She kissed her lips and a sparkling breath of air passed from her into her daughter's mouth. Tiashi the Mystic fell to the floor limp. Dead.

Ashley the Mystic knelt down and kissed her mother's lifeless lips. A single tear ran its course down her cheek.

"Yes, it is time."

***

Gray mist covered the raging sea. The slight whisper of people coughing filled the damp summer air. Every seeing eye was impaired due to the gray mist brewing from the center of the Zaggamon Sea.

Ashley the Mystic strained her almond brown eyes to see through the mysterious gray mist. She wiped the sweat from her golden forehead as she drew a deep sigh because of the fierce heat. Steam from the sea made the atmosphere terribly humid, nearly unbearable. The air was stuffy and almost unbreathable. Ashley the Mystic pulled her thick black hair to the back of her head and braided the ebony silk into a single braid. She wore a long flowing black hooded robe that covered her entire form. Her skin was the color of the purest gold molded by the hand of a great craftsman. On every one of her fingers, she wore a black onyx ring and her oval shaped fingernails were as black as the midnight shy. Her face was decorated by natural beauty. To put makeup upon such a face would insult the Father of Creation.

The Mystic moved across the seashore with the grace of a dancer. She peered deep into the mist to discover what was causing the heavy fog and insufferable heat. Ashley the Mystic walked closer to the sea until her delicate feet were caressed by the boiling water. She didn't seem to feel the heat of the water. No sign of discomfort was on her face. The Mystic walked into the sea at a very slow pace. As she walked, she raised her hands above her head and her arms began to gyrate in a series of gestures. A low moaning noise came from the sea as Ashley the Mystic started to chant incomprehensible words. The moan from the sea became higher and higher.

The people, watching from the seashore, began to back away as they held their ears to shield themselves from the horrible noise. Fright distorted their faces and concern for their lives entered their minds.

Ashley put her arms down and refrained from her mysterious chant. The Mystic's feet rose to the surface of the water and she began to walk on the water.

In the middle of the sea, a whirlpool formed. The water raised into the air like an enormous tower shadowing everything beneath it. In a second's time, the water tower disappeared as if it had never existed. Ashley the Mystic pointed her golden finger toward the place where the water tower had been and spoke something under her breath. The people walked closer to the sea to see what was transpiring. The heavy fog lifted.

Out of the sea climbed an unimaginable creature. The monster was a woman. Not an ordinary woman but a beast with evil running through its very visible blue veins. The creature stood on the water and smiled wickedly at Ashley the Mystic.

The beast was about six and a half feet tall. Her skin was as white as baby powder in the snow. Her skin color had no life in it. No human could possibly possess it. The beast had long black hair which fell to the water. Her hair covered her breast and was held together by a silver broach located where her naval should have been. It fell to the water between her long slender legs covering her nakedness.

On the end of her fingers and toes were long black talons which curved upward ending in a razor sharp tip. The beast's eyes were the most alarming. They were endless black pools of dread, solid black with no hit of an iris, which revealed the innate evil of her rotten soul. Her black crusted lips curled as she stared into the Mystic's eyes.

"Why are you here Babylon? What do you want from my land?" The Mystic asked as the people of her land shivered with terror.

They held one another close and waited attentively for what was going to happen next.

"You have what I desire. The seals have been broken and the world is in chaos. The Father of Creation has changed his prophecy and he decided to let Apollyon and I run amuck for a time more."

"Liar! The prophecies do not change!" Ashley the Mystic screamed.

The she-demon laughed. "You claim to be wise but you've made a grave mistake! While you were receiving your power and being baptized into the new position of mystic, I abducted the purest of the Elect and I plan to sacrifice him in the dark one's name if the Father won't give me my kingdom."

"You are a fool Babylon! Your kingdom is not of this world. It is in the pit where you shall rot for eternity."

Babylon cackled, "How can you damn me witchling? Your power is not of light."

"My heart is not of darkness," the Mystic retorted with a shiver in her voice. Behind her eyes revealed a tinge of guilt for being a wielder of witchcraft. She knew that she was no child of light but she also knew that no good deed went unnoticed. Despite her inherited practice of necromancy, her desire to do what was good always preceded her.

The beast walked towards the shore but Ashley the Mystic blocked her path. The Mystic stood firm. She held out her hand and Babylon came to a halt. Ashley the Mystic had to find a way to rescue the saint and take him back to safety.

"Where is he?" Ashley screamed. Tiny waves formed at her feet. The rings on her fingers glistened in the sunlight.

"Here." Babylon chuckled as she bent low and pulled a man out of the water. The man had eyes full of fire and fearless faith. His hair was like sheep's wool, curly and thick. His skin was the color of polished copper. Babylon held him tightly around the neck and bound his hands and feet with magical thorns.

"All you have to do to save him is to give me the *Chronicles of Mystics* and I will return him back to the Father's temple," Babylon crowed.

Ashley the Mystic reached under her robe and retrieved the book.

"You are not worthy! Never will I allow such formidable power to reach your hands," she yelled while pointing to the scantily clad man held within Babylon's grasp. "Release him."

Babylon dropped the man but before he could hit the sea, a flock of angels materialized and caught his weakened body; then, bore him away.

Babylon dashed across the sea on weightless feet and grabbed at the book. She hissed with frustration as the Mystic tossed the book around in front of her.

Ashley the Mystic chanted a small entreaty. She asked the secular powers that be to bring her mother's spirit near. A wind brushed Ashley's ear. It tickled gently. Ashley felt a tingling on the back of her neck. She felt the presence of an invisible force. A small voice whispered. It was her mother advising her to taunt the beast and the beast will destroy itself.

Babylon was engulfed in fury. Fury was what the Mystic wanted. Ashley the Mystic knew that too much evil and frustrated anger would destroy itself. The Mystic toyed with the horrible beast. She concealed the book and wrestled with the she-demon. Ashley the Mystic was physically stronger but Babylon was more vicious. Babylon left bloody scratches on Ashley's skin, deep bite marks in her flesh, and dark bruises on her face. The Mystic was relentless and wrestled the beast with all of her might. Babylon roared with anger. Suddenly, Babylon broke free from Ashley the Mystic's grip. Babylon's white skin began to bubble and blister. Her skin tone became fire red. Ashley the Mystic egged her on by disappearing and reappearing behind her. She flashed the book and hid it again.

"Give me the book!" Babylon yelled as she leapt toward the Mystic. Ashley the Mystic was too quick for her. The people on the shore looked at the spectacle and laughed despite of their fear. "Give me the book!" she screamed as her blistering flesh exploded into nothingness.

Ashley the Mystic turned away and walked slowly with heavy and weary steps to the seashore; water splashing high with every step. Her tattered flesh and energy drained body fell flat upon the sand.

"Forgive me for my wickedness. Do not let death claim me in my impurity," she uttered under her breath.

"You are worthy," a strident voice uttered. "Cast away your sorcery and serve me. Your heart is humbled and your intentions are pure but your practices are depraved.   Cast off your iniquities and become what you are destined to become."

"I denounce it all. Forgive me!" Tears dampened the sand and caused the grains to cling to her eyelids.

"My child you are forgiven. You are no longer Ashley but you shall be called Urial, for I am your light."

Luminosity fell from Paradise and engulfed Ashley the Mystic. When the light lifted, two golden wings protruded from her back and fluttered making a soft humming noise. A bright golden halo levitated over her head like a circle of sparkling sunbeams. Urial fell to her knees in praise to the Father of Creation as the people all followed her example.

The making of an angel.

THE MAN DIDN'T GET GRANDDADDY

"I never thought I would live to tell this story. The events I went through these past few weeks were a lot more than I could handle," said the old man as he pulled the hospital sheet across his chest. He pointed to a cup of water on a nearby table. A young brown hand handed it to him. "Thanks. Well, you really want to know the reason for my heart attack boy?"

"Yes granddaddy."

"What did your mother tell you?" The old man focused his wrinkled eyes on the boy.

"She said that you were just old and people get sick sometimes."

"Well that's true but that's not the reason why my heart played a trick on me. I was frightened. I was scared so bad that my heart couldn't take it."

"Scared of what grandpa?"

"Scared of Death."

"I don't understand," the boy said with a look of confusion on his handsome chocolate face. "How could death scare you to death?" His eyes spread wide.

The old man laughed a hearty laugh. He laughed so hard that he hurt himself. He grabbed his chest and tried to refrain from laughing.

"Ha-ha boy, you are something else. Well I saw... Okay, I'll tell you the whole story."

The old man pushed a button so he could raise the bed into a sitting position. He ran his brown wrinkled fingers through his silver hair. The old man's eyes stared deeply into his grandson's and he took a deep breath.

"Two Mondays ago, I was walking home from Joe's Barber shop. That Joe is a mess," the old man laughed. "He was talking about how Mike Tyson was the best fighter ever. What a nut! Ali was the best by far!" The old man shook his head. "Anyway, I left the shop. I walked through the old cotton field and got to my house in about ten minutes. When I opened the door, I walked to my favorite chair, sat down, and lit a sweet maple cigar. I sat there about half an hour sipping sugar water when I put out the cigar and I fell into a deep sleep. After a while, I opened my eyes and Ruby was standing in front of me."

"But grandma's dead, granddaddy!" the little boy interrupted. "How could you see her?"

"Well, I don't know but I did. Sometimes logic just can't explain everything"

"What's logic?"

"Things that are supposed to make sense. And, me seeing your grandma wasn't logical."

"It sure wasn't. That didn't make sense at all!" the boy agreed.

"You're a smart young'un." The old man smiled and rubbed the boys head.

"Grandpa you are going to mess up my fade!" the boy squealed.

"An arrogant little son of a gun too," the old man laughed. "But back to my story. Ruby walked over to me and ran her fingers through that pretty hair she had. I just sat there in shock staring into her big black eyes. Her skin was still as pretty and smooth as black satin. My God, she was the most beautiful woman in the universe. Her skin was the product of rich African blood. My God, she was pretty. She wore her favorite apron with the yellow chicken on the front of it. She smelled of rose water." The old man had tears in his eyes.

"I miss grandma too. She was pretty."

"Was! Still is! That woman made every man weep with frustration. When she was young, she won every beauty pageant at the country fair. She was truly a southern belle. A matter of fact, I think that term referred to her," he yelled.

"What's a southern belle?"

"It is woman from the south who is beautiful and sweet."

"Okay. Mama must be a southern belle then."

"She sure is boy. Anyhow, Ruby spoke to me with that sweet slow Georgia drawl of hers. You remember her voice don't you? She spoke like she was singing a song. Like every word lasted a minute long. She told me that I would be with her soon if I don't watch out. I asked her what to watch out for but she just disappeared. I was worried all day and for the next couple of days. That was the last time I saw Ruby. When Wednesday rolled around, I went on my regular evening walk. You know I have to keep these old bones in shape. It was about six o'clock. I had to wait until the day cooled a little. The sun gets too hot when age is on you. Anyway," he paused. "I was walking down the cotton field path and heading to the street when I saw this big crowd around Joe's Barber Shop. Well, I went ahead to see what was going on. Joe had just been robbed. Could you believe that? What happened to the way things use to be? It ain't but a hand full of people in this tiny town and one of these fools around here stealing like a fox in a hen house." Anger was in the old man's eyes. "That just pisses me off!" he yelled.

"Granddaddy you said a bad word."
"Sorry."
"That's okay," the boy forgave him and rubbed his grandfather's big hand.
"Thanks boy." He smiled.
"Anyway, as I walked away, I looked into the alley between June's sewing machine shop and June Bug's rib shack. I saw this man. He was wearing all black and his skin was as black as tar too. I tell you, if it was night, all you could see would be eyes and teeth. The man looked at me and tipped his hat. He had the weirdest eyes!"
"What was wrong with his eyes?"
"They were yellow."
"Yellow?"
"Yes yellow."

"How can eyes be yellow?" the boy asked in disbelief.

"His was. And when I looked in them, I just felt a chill go down my spine and the man just disappeared. A second later, I heard someone call my name. I turned around and old Tom told me that Joe was dead. Old Joe dead! I couldn't believe it. The robber made him have another stroke. I just stood there in awe!"

"What does awe mean?"

"It means that I was surprised. God, I was hurt. That old nut was one of my closest friends. We were sharecroppers when we were young. We worked the same land. I helped him build his barbershop with these two old hands. He helped me pay for school. I was the only colored doctor in this little town for almost twenty years. I loved that old fool."

"That's a bad word grandpa."

"Sorry. I went to the funeral on Saturday. It was beautiful. That night I sat in my favorite chair and Joe appeared to me. I almost wet my britches! Joe told me not to let *Him* get me. I asked who *Him* was but old Joe just disappeared like one watermelon at a family reunion."

"Wow. This story is weird."

"I'm not finished!" the old man raised his voice slightly.

"Sorry."

"Forgiven. Two days later I went to visit Rose. Now that is a crazy gal. She tickles me. Every day she made me laugh."

"Wasn't that your girlfriend grandpa?"

"Heck naw boy! You crazy? She's a Nawlins gal. New Orleans in case you didn't know. A Creole gal. You mess around with one of those Creole gals and they'll bury your drawers in the yard and you will never be able to leave their house. I tell you the truth. She was pretty as a peach but as crazy as a loon."

"What's a loon."

"A lunatic."

"What's that?"

"A crazy person."

"She was pretty when she was young. I saw some of her pictures when she came over to your house the last time," said the boy.

"When she was young? Hell! She's a fox now!"

"Grandpa you said a...."

"Sorry. Anyway, as I walked up to her door, I saw the same dark fellow sitting on her porch. As I walked up the steps, he lifted his hat and disappeared. I walked into Rose's house and there she was laying on the floor dead. I cried like a baby. The doctor said that she had an asthma attack. I miss the old goose. I went to her funeral on that Tuesday. She was as beautiful in death as she was in life."

"Did you love her grandpa?"

"I guess I did."

"More than grandma?"

"Never more than grandma."

"I loved your girlfriend too grandpa. She was nice."

"Yes she was." The old man paused in reflection. "Anyway, on that Thursday I went to see the doctor. I wanted to know that I was okay. I realized that I am getting up in age and time is winding down."

"What do you mean about time is winding down?"

"I'm getting older and I don't have a lot of time."

"You are only ninety-one. You have plenty of time."

"Thanks! I need to hear that." The old man laughed aloud. "The doc told me that I was as healthy as a horse so I felt a little better. The next day, I was sitting in my chair when I heard the young woman across the street yelling like a banshee!"

"What's a......" the boy was cut off.

"A ghost that screams real loud."

"You've heard one?"

"No but your grandma used to sound like one when she yelled at me. God, I miss her loud mouth. It used to sound like a train whistle or a pig squealing 'cause it was so loud."

"How long has she been gone?"

"Five years, six months, and seven days."

"You do miss her."

"Yes I do." The old man's eyes watered a tiny bit. He wiped his eyes quickly and continued. "Anyhow, the lady was yelling and carrying on so much that I walked out onto my porch and looked out across the street. The ambulance came screaming down the street and the paramedics went into the house. They came out with her little boy on a stretcher. They were carrying him to the ambulance when I saw the man in the black come and touch the boy's hand. The boy died that second and the man looked at me, tipped his hat, and disappeared.

"Are you talking about Rico?" the boy's voice was shaking.

"Yes boy. He choked to death on a piece of peppermint." The old man put his arms around his grandson as the boy cried aloud.

"He was my friend. I will never eat peppermint again."

"It could kill ya!" the old man added. "I decided to go to church that Sunday 'cause I had to make sure I was right with God. I can't be getting tortured by some half jackass with horns for eternity. It's too hot down there and you know how I feel about the heat. I been done put a whipping on the old Devil with a sugarcane pole for trying to stick me with a pitchfork."

"Grandpa you said a........"

"A bad word. I'm sorry. Your mother sure taught you well. Anyhow....."

"What does eternity mean?" the boy asked.

"It means forever."

"Oh. Yeah forever is a long time to be hot."

"Anyway, I put on my brown suit with my hat and newly shined shoes. I was as sharp as a tack. I looked like I should have been singing at a juke joint. I went to church and had a good-o-time. The spirit was moving and the preacher was preaching. If my knees weren't so bad, I might have done the holy dance."

"Ha-ha. I couldn't see you dancing grandpa. You too old."

"Too old! I can still cut the rug!" the old man laughed. "I felt good that day so I went to Burt and Sadie's house for dinner. My, that food of hers can put hair on your chest. It was as good as gold! Woo-wee! That food was good. We had some collard greens, candy yams, corn bread, fried chicken, potato salad, homemade biscuits, lemonade, and some good old rice pudding. That woman still cooks like she cooking for the whole chain gang. She still gets around well for an eighty-six year old. Still a pretty gal too. Burt is a lucky nut. I stayed over there 'til about eight and I made my way home. Of course I had to kiss Sadie's sweet cheek and talk about Burt's bad knees before I left. That is a good man. You here me? A good man. We served in the army together. My dearest friend on this earth. We are two of a kind. I am just a year younger than him. We met Sadie and Ruby at the same time. They were two of the most beautiful creatures God made. My God, I loved Ruby." He paused in reflection then continued, "Anyway, on my way home I noticed that dark fellow was following me. I walked a little faster and got to my door. I looked behind me and the man tipped his hat and disappeared. I then began to realize who this fellow was."

"Who was he?"

"The Grim Reaper himself," the old man said.

"Who?" the boy asked.

"Death."

"Death ain't no man."

"How do you know?" the old man asked, raising his eyebrow.

"I don't." The little boy lifted and dropped his shoulders. He crossed his arms and shook his head.

"Well hush up!" The old man waved the boy away. "Come Monday morning, more bad news. I was watching the evening news when I saw a shooting on TV. I be damned if that wasn't that dark man on the scene of the crime. He seemed to see me through the TV and tipped his hat at me. I almost crapped in my britches."

"Grandpa if you don't stop saying bad words I'm gonna tell mama.

"And what is mama gonna do?"

" I don't know. I'm just gonna tell."

"Well sorry," the old man said in a very annoyed voice. "Well, Wednesday was the day that changed my life. I was sitting in my chair when that dark fellow appeared in front of me. I was scared to death. I was more scared than a black man at a Klan meeting. He walked over to me. His yellow eyes were glowing like fire and he reached out his hand. A sinister smile crossed his lips.

"What does sinister mean?"

"Evil!!!" the old man yelled. "He reached out his hand and put it on my head. He was as cold as ice. My chest began to throb with pain and a golden light fell between me and the dark fellow. A voice said, 'It's not his time,' and the dark one took his hand away and disappeared. Luckily you and your mama came over just in time and called the ambulance and here I am. I've been lying up in this hospital for three days."

"I'm glad he didn't get you."

"Me too!"

The door opened and both grandfather and grandson turned towards the door. A tall and shapely golden skin woman walked in. She had a beautiful and kind face.

"Mama!" the boy screamed and ran to hug the woman. "The man didn't get granddaddy."

"What man?"

"That the man with the yellow eyes."

"Daddy! What have you been telling him?" the pretty woman asked with a suspicious smile on her face.

"I told him about my heart attack and how old Death couldn't get me," the old man said proudly with his hand in a fist on his hip and his mouth pursed tight.

"He sure couldn't!" she said as she put the boy down and walked over to her father and kissed him on the mouth. "He sure couldn't.

TWO BY THE SEA

"As I sit here and watch the sunset, I reminisce on all I have been through. Thank you God for allowing me to see another day. How I savor the fresh scent of salt water and the feel of waves caressing my toes. I wasn't supposed to be here. I cannot believe that I made it to see the glorious sky once again. It is funny how you neglect the world around you until you realize it may be gone forever," the woman spoke softly as she leaned back and let her palms sink into the soft damp sand. "I am so grateful." A tear ran down her chestnut cheek. "I am so grateful."

Behind her an old man walked the beach. He spied the middle aged woman sitting on the sea shore alone and began walking towards her. He took his time as he walked; his decrepit form hunched over and slightly trembling. Liver spots were sprinkled all over his pale pink skin. He shuffled behind the dark haired woman and tapped her on the shoulder.

"Excuse me miss," he apologetically said when he noticed that she was startled. "You seem a little unhappy."

"Oh, not at all. I am in bliss really." She sighed. "Won't you sit down." She pointed to the pile of sand next to her.

"Thanks," he said as he struggled to sit down. He almost lost his balance until she caught his arm and helped lower him down.

"Thanks," he said with a sigh of relief. "It is such a lovely night. What is a lovely young lady like yourself doing out here?" he asked as he observed her torn shirt and dingy jean shorts. There were traces of blood all over her.

"I am hardly young." She smiled and shook her head. "I am forty-six years old."

"You are a baby! I am ancient by comparison!"

"What a blessing!" she exclaimed. "Life is such a precious gift. I used to worry about getting old until I realized that when a person stops aging they are dead." She laughed quietly and lightly tapped his arm in a playful manner.

"We all are blessed." He smiled and put his hand on her shoulder. His kind face glowed in the bright moonlight. "Why are you here child?" he inquired with deep concern.

"I have no where else to be. I have no place to go. I have no home." She bowed her head and sprinkled sand over her feet. The sound of the ocean roared in her ears. She took a deep breath and released.

"Do you want to talk?" He adjusted his legs. His blue gray hair glistened in the moonlight. His clear gray eyes seemed to have a story of their own. A peaceful aura surrounded him. Tranquility resided in his smile.

"Sure." She looked at him as if she had known him all her life. "You look strangely familiar to me. Do I know you?" she asked, staring into those mystical eyes of his.

"We all know each other." He leaned back on his elbows. "Child, you have to understand that we all are connected to one another. We are all branches growing out of the tree of God. We are connected to one another by spirit and divine relation. We are children of Adam and Eve, sisters and brothers. We all are a part of each other and everyone feels everyone's pain. That is why I came to you."

She laughed. "What are you talking about?!"

"I am talking about life."

"That all sounds good but I am a realist. I don't believe much in things I cannot see or understand. I wasn't really sure about God until I reached the nadir of my life. I was never the one who entertained the idea of supernatural beings," she said.

"Do you believe in ghosts?" he asked with an austere expression.

"No. Why?" Chills ran down her neck. She became a little uneasy. She ran her hand over her hair and looked at the ocean.

"Let me try to explain." He smiled. "Fear not my child. There is nothing to be afraid of." He gave her a soothing smile. "Young one, ghosts are souls who are trapped within the realm of reality. Sometimes they don't even realize they are deceased."

"Why are you talking about this?" She began to get up, full of annoyance and vexation.

"Please don't." he pleaded. He grabbed her hand and held it tightly. A faint warmth pulsated through him and entered her hand. Calm rested upon her. She remained seated.

"Don't leave. I do not want to drive you away. I'm just telling you why I seem so familiar to you," he said.

"Are you telling me you are a ghost?" Her eyes bucked.

He gave a hardy laugh. "I didn't say that. Take it easy. Why should you be afraid anyway?"

"Because that would mean that you are dead."

"What is death but another stage of life?" He smiled. "Do not fear death. In death you will not miss a sunset or a raindrop. You will only miss your love ones and that will only be for a short time. It all fades."

"You are scaring me." She was trembling.

"Don't be." He held her hand.

"How do you know these things?" she asked.

"I have been around for a long time. I have witnessed many things in my lifetime."

She sat back at ease; lost once again in his crystal gray eyes. She gave him a weary smile and said, "Tell me more."

"Memory is the only thing that links us is to the world of reality. Once that is gone, we are on the way to the plane of nonexistence."

"Nonexistence?"

"We exist, but not to the world. We are just wondering around helping others until

Peace Day. Like angels, we become like angels, total spiritual beings whose only purpose is to serve God."

"Peace Day?" Her left eyebrow rose and she turned her torso to face him. She was intrigued now.

"That is what you call Judgment Day." He smiled again.

She smiled back at him. Her nerves were calming down. The cool breeze from the ocean gave her chills. She shivered.

"Cold is in the mind. Warm yourself," the old man said.

"How?" she questioned.

"Speak it away. There is immense power in words."

"Cold be gone!" She looked unsure. She still shivered.

"Faith my dear," he said. "Ask and it shall be given. Seek and you will find."

She closed her eyes and took a deep breath. "Cold be gone." At once the breeze ceased. Her body reclaimed its natural body temperature. She was astonished.

"See, it is easy." He laughed aloud. "It is amazing!" He clapped his thick wrinkled hands. The dark blue polo shirt he wore ruffled as he moved. The bottom of his plaid shorts were getting wet by the tide.

"See how faith changes things! Why are you out here? Why haven't you reclaimed your life?" he asked.

Anger flashed across her face.

"I am just happy to be alive!" she snapped. "Things have been difficult for me. I am blessed just to be sitting here talking to you!"

"Don't just be content with mere life. The life you live is nothing more than the stage before the next life. You have to cherish each stage or the next stage will only get worse. How you live now is preparing your soul for eternity. We make our own heaven or hell with the choices we make."

"You seem so wise yet I am motivated to think that you may be insane."

"Insanity is an unstable state of mind. I am at peace. I do not even comprehend insanity." He smiled once again, not offended by her comment. "Why are you here? Homeless? Hopeless?"

"A few weeks ago I left my ex-husband. He misused and abused me for years. I tried to leave in peace but he refused to let me go. So, I decided to pack a couple of my things and stay at a friend's house. When I arrived home, all of the locks were changed. My so-called friends would not give me shelter. He is a very powerful man. He is a senator. I would have never thought he would be so cruel." She wiped a tear from her eye.

"What do you mean you thought he wouldn't be so cruel? He abused you physically didn't he?"

"Yes."

"How much more cruel does he have to be?"

"I know. I know!" she snapped. "I just didn't think he would make me homeless. I loved that man! My family turned their backs on me because of him. They thought he was too old and him being in politics didn't help." She paused. "I put up with years of infidelity, abuse mentally and physically, and he threw me out on the street! I was hurt and angry so I tried to make him surrender to extortion. I hired a detective a few years back. I had pictures of him committing adultery and I was going public if he didn't give me money and the house. He refused and he put a contract out on my life. I look like this because I have been running for a week and a half. I have been getting by. By the skin of my teeth! Last night the hit man caught up to me. We struggled and I am so glad that I survived." She let the tears come.

"Have you tried to ask for help?" he asked.

"No one seems to acknowledge me. Now I know how the unfortunate feel when people look down their noses at them and treat them subhuman. I feel as if I am no more than a seashell on a pile of sand to these people." Her voice cracked with pain and humiliation. "He ruined me for life!" she spat the words out like bile in her mouth. "People pass me like I am not here."

"Maybe you are not!" His face went suddenly serious. "Think about the struggle. What happened?"

"Don't be absurd." Her lips curled downward in resentment.

"Calm down and think about the struggle. I am only here to help. Keep your anger at bay."

"Well," She cleared her throat and sat up straight. "I was sitting on the curb by a busy intersection. I had just finished eating at a nearby shelter and I was contemplating my next move. Suddenly, I got a very uneasy feeling so I hid in a nearby alley. Don't ask me why I chose a dark place like that. I wasn't thinking. I just knew danger was near. I felt so strongly that I had to hide myself. Anyway, I kneeled next to a trash can and peered out into the darkness. Minutes went by and I thought I was safe. I let out a loud sigh and then a man attacked me. He bolted out of the darkness and brutally assaulted me. All I felt were heavy blows against my face and chest but I fought back. From what I could make out, he had a knife and we struggled and struggled. I felt great pain and I felt wetness cover me. It was too dark to see anything. Then, I broke free. I don't know how but I was free from him and the pain left me. All I know is that I escaped and I ran from the alley and I have been here since then thanking God for my life."

"Come with me," he requested. He stood up and offered her his hand.

She took it and stood up.

The old man saw a young couple walking down the beach.

"Excuse me!" he yelled. The couple walked on as if they heard nothing. "Excuse me!" The couple walked on. The old man ran in front of them and jumped up and down.

They walked on. He smiled and walked back to the lady. "Try it."

She did the same thing and went unnoticed.

"What is going on?" She turned to the old man for answers. Fear grabbed a hold of her heart.

"Welcome to death. It isn't as bad as you thought it would be huh?"

"You mean?" She panicked. "I'm dead. You're dead?" Her eyes stretched wide, her mouth formed a perfect "o", and her nose flared.

"As a door knob." He smiled. "Calm down. I was sent here to make your trip to the other place a little less lonely." He grabbed a hold of her hand, smiled, and vanished.

She looked around for him. He was no where to be found. She felt his invisible hand on her arm and she was pulled into the void with him.

"Continue to give thanks because it only gets better," his pleasant voice echoed through the salty air and floated away with the wind.